MURDER IN ITALY

A Midwest Cozy Mystery - Book 6

BY

DIANNE HARMAN

Published by: Dianne Harman
www.dianneharman.com

Interior, cover design and website by
Vivek Rajan

ISBN: 9781792199349

CONTENTS

ACKNOWLEDGMENTS

For Tom. I remember everything about our trip to Italy. Thank you for making this wonderful country come alive for me.

Win FREE Paperbacks every week!

Go to www.dianneharman.com/freepaperback.html and get your FREE copies of Dianne's books and favorite recipes immediately by signing up for her newsletter.

Once you've signed up for her newsletter you're eligible to win three paperbacks. One lucky winner is picked every week. Hurry before the offer ends!

PROLOGUE

Bruno Lombardi leaned back in his chair with a satisfied sigh and looked out over his Sardinian vineyard and the bright azure blue sea beyond it. The tasting days were the best days of the year, and today was the first of those extra special days.

"This is the life, eh, Chiari?" he said. "The vineyard manager said this is the best year for grapes he's ever seen, here or anywhere else. The wine will be fabulous. Just fabulous, I'm sure of it."

"Hmm," his wife Chiari said. She fiddled with her long black hair and didn't look at all as enthusiastic as Bruno.

"Wine Spectator has already written about it," he said. "And all the other magazines, of course. This year's wine is really attracting a buzz."

Chiari was as stunningly beautiful as she had always been. But her perfectly-lipsticked mouth did not stretch into a smile when, in response to her husband's enthusiastic statement, she said, "That's nice," and continued staring off into space.

Bruno was starting to get annoyed. "Aren't you happy about it?"

"Yes," she said with a sigh. "But all I hear about is wine. While I am proud of you, very much so, sometimes I wish…" Her big brown

1

eyes scanned his face. "Oh, never mind."

Bruno softened a little. "Sometimes you wish what?"

"You're always so busy. Let's not let the years pass us by until we're invalids, stuck in this enormous mansion. Let's travel, before we get too old to go anywhere."

"Hmm."

"You've always said we'll go to the United States someday, but it never happens. Why don't we make it this year?"

"Yes, that would be nice, dear." Bruno looked at his watch. "First I have to meet with the vineyard manager to discuss what we'll concentrate on for the coming year. That's a priority, but we'll talk about going to the United States later."

With that, he got up, leaving Chiari on the sweeping veranda to watch the sunset dip below the sea, just as she had done so many times before, alone. Bruno looked back momentarily, only to find her glowering in his direction. *Women,* he thought. *Always far too demanding.*

Chiari was the most provided-for woman in all of Sardinia. She could have a sumptuous feast for breakfast, lunch and dinner, and stay in a different bedroom each night of the month, if she wanted, there were so many. She had designer dresses from Milan, Paris, and New York sent to her, diamonds from Botswana, and expensive paintings from all over the world. What more could she possibly want?

Bruno went inside the house to see if the preparations had been made for the tasting. He was a little early, but he was too excited to wait patiently. He wanted to be in the wine cellar at the very first possible moment after everything had been organized.

He strode through the marble-floored salon toward the back rooms.

"Well," he said authoritatively to his vineyard manager, who was just coming up from the cellar. "I trust everything's ready?"

"All prepared, yes, sir," the vineyard manager said. "Now, before the grand moment, do you have a few minutes to speak about our plans for the coming year?"

"You know I always have time to talk about wine," Bruno said. "Let's go into the salon."

"Yes, sir. What would you like to drink?"

"Water, obviously," Bruno said sharply. "You know I don't want to compromise my palate."

"Of course, sir."

They spoke about the upcoming year for quite a while. Bruno was in his element when he was talking and planning about wine.

"I'm sorry, sir, but I have to head off for my daughter's school play," the vineyard manager said. "Everything is set up as usual in the cellar. I look forward to hearing your feedback tomorrow."

Bruno smiled and shook his hand heartily. "Yes, absolutely. I am sure it will be as spectacular as we... and the rest of the world... imagine."

"Indeed!"

Bruno paused at the doorway leading to the cellar, savoring every moment. These were perhaps the best of his life. The moments he most cherished. He opened the door, seeing the soft golden lights he'd chosen for ambience, lighting up the cellar with a warm glow.

He went down the stairs and soon the most pleasing view came into sight – the table. His table. His new release table. It was a sturdy, old-fashioned heavy table that had come from his grandmother's kitchen. He'd loved eating at it as a little boy, his dark-haired head barely reaching high enough for him to shovel forkfuls of ravioli into his mouth.

Chiari had said it didn't go with the sleek white décor she'd picked out for the kitchen, so it wouldn't fit in there. Bruno had been furious at first, until he'd realized that his pride of place was not in the kitchen, but in his wine cellar. So there the old table sat along his passion, his endless sea of bottles of wine.

He approached the table and saw that all of the items he needed were there – the chair, the pen, the paper, a crystal wine glass, and an open bottle of wine. He didn't like to have to work with corks when he was tasting a new release.

It was a Cannonau di Sardegna, like a fifth of the other wines produced on the island. But his wine was one in a million, he told himself as he took his seat. He was certain it would be raved about in respected wine publications worldwide.

After he was seated, he poured the wine, savoring the trickling sound he so loved to hear. He smelled it – a gorgeously rich berry smell, with a most pleasing scent of spice mingling in with it. He swirled the rich red wine in his glass, watching it create its own little whirlpool. Then he sipped it.

Yes, he thought as he savored the sumptuous meeting of spice and fruit. *It is exquisite!*

As he picked his glass up for another sip, the room around him became a blur. He felt himself falling sideways off his chair. Both Bruno and the chair crashed on the floor with a loud thud. The wine glass in his hand smashed on the floor, and wine poured out like so much blood, gathering in a small pool on the flagstone floor.

Bruno was dead.

CHAPTER ONE

Kat Denham looked out the window of the plane as they made their descent into JFK airport in New York. She and Blaine Evans, her district attorney husband, clinked their champagne glasses together.

"It looks like a little toy town from up here," Blaine said with a laugh.

"It does, doesn't it?" Kat replied, snuggling into his shoulder. "I'm so glad we're getting away for a while. As much as I love our life together in Kansas, it's great to have a change of scenery."

"I couldn't agree more," Blaine said. "Don't get me wrong, I love being the District Attorney, but I'm looking forward to having a break from all the responsibilities of the job. We'll come back refreshed and recharged."

"Absolutely, but I already miss Lacie, Jazz, and Rudy." Kat's daughter, Lacie, who was studying to be a child psychologist, was back in their hometown of Lindsay, Kansas. She lived in an apartment with her boyfriend Tyler, but they'd temporarily moved into Kat and Blaine's home to housesit and take care of Kat's beloved dogs, Jazz and Rudy.

"I'm sure they'll miss you, too," Blaine said. "But Jazz and Rudy will have a great time with Lacie and Tyler. They'll be so spoiled by the time we get back, you won't recognize them."

"That's probably true," Kat said. Lacie had a propensity for feeding the dogs far too many treats and picking up little toys from the store for them each time she went shopping. "They'll love it. It's just that it's been a long time since I've been so far away from them."

Blaine squeezed her hand. "Don't forget, you need to take care of yourself, too. Trust me, you're going to thoroughly enjoy our trip."

Kat smiled. "I know that. Of course, being Deborah's matron of honor is the most important thing on the trip's itinerary. I wouldn't miss that for the world." Deborah was a very close friend of Kat's. She'd been the head of the Sex Therapy Department at the university in Lindsay, but after a coed was murdered near the campus, she'd gone on a sabbatical to Italy and divorced her husband. It was meant to be a short trip, but since she'd snagged both a plum job and a wonderful man, it only made sense to stay.

She was now the head of the Sex Therapy Department at a university near Florence, and the fiancée of Luigi Giordano, a successful winemaker with a private plane and a house that was only a couple turrets short of being a castle. He was kind and attentive, according to Deborah, and Kat was so happy for her. Deborah was such a wonderful woman, and after everything she'd been through, Kat felt she absolutely deserved this newfound happiness.

"Not only are we going to enjoy Italy," Kat said, looking down at New York with a smile on her lips, "I'm also planning on enjoying New York in style."

"Not a problem," Blaine said.

"Well, it certainly started with this flight," Kat said. She settled back into her luxurious pod seat. "I can't believe we're flying first class."

Kat had never really splurged on luxuries. It was Blaine who had persuaded her. "I want to treat you," he'd said. "You deserve the best." He was very free with money when it came to making other people feel happy. He'd inherited an insane amount when his parents had died and much of that money had been donated by him to charities and non-profits. However, there was still a lot left for him to spend as he wished.

Kat had let him take care of everything, from the flights to the hotel to their itinerary. If the flight from Kansas City to New York City was any indication, she couldn't wait to see what else he'd come up with.

The landing was smooth, as was their journey through the airport to the taxi stand. "To the Four Seasons," Blaine said to the driver, and before long they were pulling up at the grand entrance.

"Oh my," Kat said, with a short intake of breath.

Her amazement only increased as they stepped inside the lobby. It was positively palatial, with grand pillars standing guard at each corner of the atrium. The ceiling was vaulted with a yellow skylight that cast warm light onto each of the gleaming marble surfaces.

She nudged Blaine as they made their way to the front desk. "Look," she whispered. "Can you believe it? There are trees... inside!"

Sure enough, there were two full-sized trees just behind the reception desk.

It didn't take long to check in and ride the elevator up to their floor. Soon they were stepping into their luxurious suite.

Kat would never have chosen the color scheme, but she loved it. Sweeping beige curtains were complemented by sleek gray furnishings. There was an enormous flat screen television in the living room, and even a gray grand piano. She wished she or Blaine knew how to play, and wondered if the hotel provided a complementary piano player as part of the room fee, which she knew must be astronomical.

Next she took a quick peek into the bathroom to see both a bath and a shower, warm-colored tiles, soft lighting, and plenty of white fluffy towels. The bedroom was wonderfully cozy, too, with mocha and beige striped curtains hanging to the floor, a king-sized bed with crisp white fresh linens, and a little reading nook with its own window looking out at the city.

Kat returned to the living room. "District Attorney Evans, what have you done?!" she asked as soon as the porter had left their bags for them. "This is simply incredible."

Blaine grinned and put his arms around Kat's waist.

"All for us, Sexy Cissy." Kat was a successful author and Sexy Cissy was the pen name she used when she wrote her steamy romance books, while she reserved her own name for her mystery books. She'd almost quit writing after her editor was murdered and quite a few people figured out that she was Sexy Cissy. Sometimes in a teasing manner Blaine called her by that name, and she liked it. It was as if her writing steamy romance novels was a little secret between the two of them.

As they both looked out the huge floor to ceiling window that showed them an impressive panorama of skyscrapers, Kat said, "That's going to look amazing tonight."

"I just hope you enjoy yourself," Blaine sid. "We need to get going, because we've only got a short time to take in as much as we possibly can."

And take it all in they did.

First they went to Central Park, where they took a horse and buggy ride, which felt magical. Next, they spent far too long at Saks 5th Avenue, browsing around all the different specialty sections of the store. Kat bought a Mulberry handbag that was on sale. She also snuck off for a while and bought Blaine a bottle of his favorite aftershave, Ralph Lauren's Polo Supreme Leather, as a surprise. It came in a lovely red bottle with gold detailing. Blaine broke into a smile when he saw it and kissed her cheek.

"Where shall we go for dinner?" Kat asked as they stepped out of Saks with their shopping bags.

"Aha, I've already taken care of that. Let's go."

They took a yellow cab, and soon they were at Le Bernardin, a well-known French restaurant. "I researched it online," Blaine said. "It got terrific reviews."

"I'm not surprised. It's been featured in a lot of magazines I've read."

To top off the evening, they headed to see the play *Wicked* at the Gershwin Theater on Broadway. Kat didn't generally care for musicals, but she thought this one was worth the acclaim it had gotten, and the music was particularly rousing. She was sure Lacie would have loved it, and made a mental note that maybe they could take a mother-daughter trip to New York sometime.

After setting a phone alarm, and requesting a wake-up call from hotel reception just in case, they fell asleep the moment their heads hit the pillow. It had been a very long, fully packed day, and they had an early flight to catch.

The next afternoon they landed in Florence just after 4:00 p.m., and cleared customs and immigration without any problems. When they walked out of the arrivals area and into the waiting area, the first person they saw was Deborah, looking fantastic in loose white linen pants and a powder blue shirt that matched her smiling eyes.

"Deborah," Kat said, beaming.

She and Deborah embraced each other in a long lingering hug.

"It's so good to see you," Deborah said, giving her a squeeze. "And you, Blaine. How was the flight?"

Deborah and Blaine kissed on each cheek.

"It was great," Kat said. "Plenty of movies to keep us occupied." She looked at the large, handsome man standing by Deborah's side, who had dark hair that was graying at the temples in quite a distinguished way. "And you must be Luigi? We've heard so much about you."

Kat and Luigi double-kissed, then Luigi shook Blaine's hand.

"I've heard a lot about you, too," he said with a deep Italian accent. "Kat Denham, author extraordinaire and unofficial super detective, and the honorable and hard-working District Attorney Blaine Evans. So glad to finally meet both of you."

"Oh, you flatter us," Kat said. *What a charming guy!* she thought.

Deborah linked arms with Kat as they left the airport, while Blaine and Luigi took the bags and walked behind them. Kat smiled when she stepped out into the warm Italian air. A gentle breeze was blowing, keeping the heat comfortable.

"Wow, the weather's great," Kat said.

Deborah smiled. "Yep. Gotta love a little sunshine every day. It makes everything seem brighter, doesn't it?"

They walked to a nearby black Mercedes Maybach parked in front of the airport terminal building, its chrome rims gleaming in the bright Italian sunlight.

"Here's our little ride home," Deborah said.

Blaine leaned over to Kat and whispered, "Do you know how much this thing costs?"

"More than our house, probably," Kat whispered back through a laugh.

"You bet," Blaine said. "It's humongous."

A large man wearing sunglasses and dressed in a police uniform was standing next to the car, as if he was guarding it. Luigi handed the man a few euros and said something in Italian.

Deborah laughed. "That's the good thing about Italy. The car is illegally parked, but this guy doesn't mind, as long as we sweeten him up a little bit."

They all got into the car, Luigi in the driver's seat.

"My vineyard is on the way to Deborah's," he said. "I thought you might like to take a look at it."

"Ooh, yes, please," Kat said. She'd heard a lot about it from Deborah, and couldn't wait to see it. It would be the first time she'd seen a vineyard in person, much less an Italian vineyard.

She settled down in the backseat next to Blaine and they interlinked their fingers and smiled at each other. She was just happy they were off on an adventure together. When Kat's husband, Lacie's father, had died, she'd never expected to find love again. But then Blaine popped up out of the blue, with his gorgeous smile that made his eyes crinkle, and his kind heart that never seemed to stop giving. She smiled and looked out the window at the brilliant blue sky as they left the airport.

Life is good, she thought.

CHAPTER TWO

"Said to be the best wine in Sardinia," Vito Rizzo read out loud to himself in a mocking tone, then threw the magazine down on the lounge next to him. "Said by whom? By imbeciles, of course!"

He was spending a lazy afternoon at Sardinia's most exclusive resort. In fact, he was in the VIP section, adults-only, where there would be no children to bother him. He hated children, especially when they shrieked and laughed and splashed in the swimming pool. The staff at the resort all knew him by name, knew exactly who he was, and catered to his every whim and desire. He was renowned for his short temper.

This might have been tempered or exacerbated by his loyal assistant (who, in reality, was a manservant, but it wasn't politically correct to call him that these days). Anyone would have thought that his assistant, Lorenzo, a lanky beanpole of a man and just 24 years old, would have quit on his first day. But he had no other job prospects and he had a young family to feed, so he wasn't stupid enough to throw away the opportunity. For some reason Vito Rizzo had taken a shine to him.

Vito lay back on his lounge, his fat belly protruding far above the rest of his body.

"You should rub some suntan lotion on your head, sir," Lorenzo dared to suggest. It had taken him a while to get up the courage to say that, since he didn't want Vito to take it the wrong way. There was a good chance he would take it as a personal insult against his balding head, and would fire back a nasty insult in return. But it was equally likely that Vito would berate him later if he did end up getting sunburned. "It will burn and hurt a lot," he added.

"How many times have I told you, boy? Suntan lotion is for cissies and tourists." It was true, he'd said that many times. Other times, he'd slapped the lotion on his head and rubbed it in, saying that Italians were ignorant for not using it, and they would all suffer horrific sun-caused deaths as a result. "Now, go get me a martini and another cigar."

"Yes, sir."

Vito lifted one of his fat legs off the lounge and lightly kicked Lorenzo as he walked past him, then he laughed raucously. "And don't fall in the pool on your way."

Lorenzo teetered dangerously close to the pool, and didn't really find it at all funny. Still, he laughed along with Vito. Sometimes, the only thing that kept him going was the image of his children sitting at an empty dinner table with rumbling bellies.

In a few minutes he returned with the requested martini and cigar.

"It's about time," Vito said as he sat up and took a big gulp of the martini. "Now, Lorenzo, you've tasted wines from that beast Bruno Lombardi, haven't you?"

Lorenzo didn't quite know how to answer. What he did know was that Vito was about to launch into a long diatribe about his rival, but should he admit to having tasted Lombardi wine? He certainly couldn't admit to enjoying them, which quite frankly, was the truth.

"Well, I tasted them before I started working for you, sir," he said carefully.

Vito laughed. "Good answer. Now, you tell me, Lorenzo. Do you really think he deserves to badmouth me each time we both enter a contest? I mean, with each and every ranking? Do you think he deserves to be posing in his fancy thousand dollar suits in every magazine and slurring my name and my wine at the same time?"

"Of course not, sir," Lorenzo said, beginning to tune out. He'd heard this rant of Vito's a million times before. He sat down on the adjacent lounge, took a sip from his water bottle, and pretended to look interested.

"Exactly. Any idiot can understand that type of thing just simply isn't done." Vito furiously opened a magazine and pointed to a glossy picture. It showed Bruno Lombardi accepting some award in a very sharp tailored suit. The accompanying article stated, "*His wine sells out at the most prestigious restaurants in Italy,*" Vito growled, his face, which was already very red from his excessive sunbathing, turning purple.

"So do yours, sir," Lorenzo said quickly.

"No, no, listen to this. And I quote, '*I thank you for this most prestigious and illustrious award. I must say, though, I will not be unnecessary modest. My wines deserve to win, as they are the best in Sardinia. Indeed, the whole of Italy. No other wine from any other producer will eclipse the glory of my own, for as long as I am alive.*' I mean, he really is disgustingly arrogant, isn't he?"

Only as arrogant as you, Lorenzo thought. "Yes. He's a disgusting man," he said.

"Then!" Vito said explosively. "Then the little cockroach gets downright personal. Read what comes next. I cannot let this filth pass my lips," he said with rage as a blob of his saliva landed on the page he was reading.

Lorenzo carefully wiped it off with his sleeve. "Um... which part am I supposed to read?" he asked, wincing in readiness for Vito's annoyance, which would inevitably be aroused by the question.

Vito stabbed the page. "That part." Then he heaved his bulk back down into a prone position on the lounge. "Go on."

"*Some say that wines made by Vito Rizzo, also of Sardinia, are Lombardi's closest rivals. I asked Lombardi about this, and he laughed. "Well, I'm not worried," he said.*" Lorenzo took a quick look at Vito, who looked like he might explode with fury at any moment. "What an ignorant piece of work," he said quickly, hoping it might help.

"But he's right, isn't he, Lorenzo? He's absolutely right! He doesn't have to be worried about me, because somehow or other he's got the world and probably even his grandmother in his pocket."

"Somehow or other?" Lorenzo repeated. "Do you mean you think he's paying them off?"

"No, you idiot. You think I haven't already explored that avenue? Many of these people who write magazine articles like this one can't be bribed. They always talk about integrity and things like that. In any case, my wines are good enough to be ranked first, to beat Lombardi's. Just because he looks like some pretty mama's boy, still, even at his age, he has the press eating out of his hand. I mean, he even puts a picture of himself on the labels of wine bottles, like he's some sort of celebrity."

"I see what you mean."

"I will come in first, though. I'm not having some mama's boy discredit my life's work by posing for some dumb magazine. No siree."

"Quite right, sir."

"Stop bleating and light my cigar."

Lorenzo did so. He coughed at the strong smoke it gave off. It seemed he could never get used to it. Vito smirked.

Lorenzo let a long period of silence stretch out between them, lest he be accused of 'bleating', then ventured, "Sir, what do you plan to do?"

"What?" Vito said, as if he'd been pulled out of a deep daydream. "Nothing. Nothing. I plan to do nothing." He took a puff on his cigar, then pointed out two young beautiful women who were sunning themselves on nearby lounges. "Go get them a drink, Lorenzo. Two fruit cocktails or some such."

"Okay, sir." Lorenzo tried to keep the weariness out of his voice. Vito was always trying to meet young ladies, and 90% of them were not even remotely interested. Perhaps one in ten could rouse some interest when they were told who he was, the unspoken attraction of course being that he was worth a lot of money and was looking for a beautiful young thing to spend it on.

"Talk me up when you take them their drinks," Vito barked at him as he headed off to the bar.

CHAPTER THREE

"They've taken the whole Ossani family for fools!" Rinaldo Ossani raged.

"Calm down, calm down," Sofia said. "Diego is trying to do his homework just across the hall. I don't want him disturbed."

"Yes, yes, you are right." Rinaldo sat back down at the kitchen table and drummed his fingers on its surface in agitation.

"Let me bring you some tea," Sofia said soothingly. "Eat your bread."

She brought two steaming cups of sweet tea, and sat down across from him. Then she slathered her own piece of bread with a chocolate-hazelnut spread. "So… talk to me, brother. What happened?"

"You know I've been a loyal worker in the Lombardi vineyards for all my life. Ever since I left school I've been toiling away like a slave for them, getting paid just a pittance in return. Is that not true?"

"It is," Sofia said. "You have been a very loyal hard worker for them."

"Nobody could deny it," Rinaldo said. "I am their longest serving employee."

"Except for Gino," Sofia pointed out.

He was the man who sat in the gatehouse and opened the barrier for Bruno's visitors to drive in, and was probably pushing his mid-80s.

"Oh, of course, Gino is more of a fixture than an employee," Rinaldo said. "He will sit in that gatehouse almost forever, or at least until they find out he hasn't been breathing for a while and rigor mortis has set in."

"Don't be so morbid," Sofia said, but she couldn't help but laugh at the thought.

Rinaldo spread his own bread with the chocolate-hazelnut spread, and sipped his tea. He kept shaking his head over and over.

"You look so upset," said Sofia. "I'm really sorry, Rinaldo."

He sighed. "It's not just this. It's what that man has done to you. That is the real issue here. This latest thing is just... I don't know... the thing that pulled the pin out of the grenade."

Sofia frowned. "Don't go and do anything stupid now," she said, patting him on the arm. "Not on my account."

Rinaldo avoided her eyes. "Anyway, here's what happened. I was given incorrect instructions by the vineyard manager. He told me to cut down a certain row of grapes and throw them away, as they were surplus and no longer needed. I did what he said. Then he returns and becomes angry with me, saying I have done the wrong thing. We argue back and forth. I tell him he made a mistake. He denies it. I just think... well, it is a misunderstanding. A bad day at work."

"Hmmm."

"But no. He goes to Bruno, and comes back in a raging fit. He fires me on the spot."

Sofia shook her head sadly. "Very unfair."

"Yes, considering I've been there ten more years than the person who fired me!" Rinaldo got to his feet in anger, then sighed and sat back down again. "Sorry. If Bruno wanted me fired, he should have been man enough to come do it himself. But instead he sent his shiny new manager to do it. They both make me sick."

"Please…" Sofia said, closing her eyes. "Do not speak about Bruno like that. He is a good man."

"A good man? Please, Sofia, do you not see that he is fooling you? That you are fooling yourself?"

"Rinaldo!" Sofia was becoming tearful. "Not now, not now, please."

"That's what you always say. And I have never pushed it before. But now? Him firing me has finally made me wake up. Now I am seeing hi for what he is. Bruno does not love you, Sofia."

"Enough, please," Sofia said, staring into her half-finished cup of tea as if her life depended on it.

"I'm sorry, Sofia, but please, let's be realistic. Why do you keep believing his promises?"

Sofia stayed silent.

"He will never leave Chiari to be with you. He will never officially recognize Diego as his son. He is playing games with your mind, to keep you quiet."

"No," Sofia choked out. "He loves me. He loves his son. He just needs time."

"How much time?" Rinaldo said. "He's had thirteen years. Do you not think that is enough time for him to gather up his courage? To finally make the decision?"

"Things got complicated," Sofia said. "First, he had a stressful business deal that dragged on for a few years. How could he leave then? After that Chiari started receiving treatments for infertility and finally found out she couldn't have children. It would be cruel to abandon her in that state. Then…"

"He always has an excuse!" Rinaldo burst out.

"Not excuses," Sofia said. "Reasons. Very good reasons. When God allows, the timing will be right."

"When God allows? You don't realize, Sofia, that the only god here is Bruno! He is the one making all the decisions. And he will never decide to be with you."

"Oh," said Sofia, her eyes blazing. "So you are inside Bruno's heart are you, knowing everything that goes on inside it?"

"Bruno does not have a heart."

"Don't be ridiculous. He is a passionate, affectionate man."

Rinaldo snorted. "He is a passionate, affectionate liar."

"You don't know," said Sofia. "Nobody knows our true love."

"Exactly, nobody knows. If it was real, if he was proud of you, he would break off with Chiari and marry you. Everyone would know. As for now, it is all a dirty little secret."

"How dare you," Sofia spat. She made sure to keep her voice down, so as not to disturb Diego, but the fury in her voice was clear. "I am no one's dirty little secret. Our love is pure, sacred." She wore a searching look for a moment, then it was overtaken with one of victory. "Our love is not of this world. It is higher. This mundane world just has to catch up."

"Keep on kidding yourself," Rinaldo said tightly. "That man is scum. Stringing you along. Lying to you all these years, and now you've lost your youth sitting by the phone, begging God and Mother Mary for him to call."

Sofia paused, a lump lodged in her throat. "Why are you saying all this, Rinaldo? Do you want to hurt a woman who is already wounded?"

"No," Rinaldo said. "I want to wake you up. I want to make you see that this man is no good for you. That you should move on with your life."

"He gave me a house, Rinaldo. This beautiful, beautiful mansion of a home. It's the finest home in the village."

"That wasn't too hard to do," Rinaldo snorted. "This village is a dump."

"Okay, it is a little poor. But they treat me like a queen here."

"Because they think you will give them money."

Sofia snapped. "And how is it that I have that money, Rinaldo? Bruno sends it to me, of course. Would he do that if he did not care?"

"Yes. He wants to keep you quiet, so you won't get angry and go tell your story to Chiari and ruin his life. Or worse, the newspapers. You could ruin his whole reputation."

"And why would I want to do that? The man has been nothing but good to me."

"Madonna Mia!" Rinaldo exclaimed. "How can you be so stupid? He's playing you like a half-rate streetwalker, while Chiari lives it up like a princess."

Sofia raised her hand as if to slap him, then she froze in mid-air and hissed through her teeth. "You are so, so lucky that my son is studying in the next room. If he were not here, I would be slapping you off the walls."

Rinaldo sighed, and smiled a little. "No, you wouldn't. You know you wouldn't."

Sofia tried to stay mad, and indignantly spread another piece of bread. "I would."

"You're Mother Earth," Rinaldo said. "With the kindest, gentlest heart of anyone I know." He took her hand in his. She snatched it away. He took it again, and she sighed, but allowed him to hold it. "You're my lovely little sister. The sweetest, kindest, gentlest person there ever was. That's why I can't stand him doing this to you. I have kept quiet all these years…"

"No, you haven't. You have always poked your nose in my business."

"All right," he said. "I have made some choice comments over the years, but it is nothing compared to what I have been feeling inside. I have been seething internally, burning whenever I thought about it, and I've tried not to make it my business. But, if truth be told, he is taking the most terrible advantage of you. And of our family. Do you not see the contempt he has for all of us?"

"No," Sofia said. "He is just a very powerful man. That is how it is. We cannot control him. Mama had Papa wrapped around her little finger because he was poor, and she was from a powerful family. Okay, they were poor, too, but in the community, they were somebody She was somebody, just because of her parents. Being the daughter of an important community figure gives you a lot of power. So Papa had to fall into line and do what she said."

"He was a good man," Rinaldo said. "Not a weak one. He adored the ground Mama walked on."

"True enough," Sofia said. "But Bruno worships the ground I

walk on, too, Rinaldo. But because he has responsibilities and power and influence, he cannot show it. If he was a poor farmer, he would be here and there would be a ring on my finger. But he is stuck. He has been trapped by his position in life, by his success. It is a heartbreaking thing, but we cannot fight reality. Soon he will manage to get himself free."

"Rubbish!" said Rinaldo. "You are talking like this is some grand love story. Like you are Juliet and he is Romeo. Do you not see how you are fooling yourself?"

"No." Sofia stood up, increasingly agitated. "Wait there."

She left the room and soon came back with Diego. He looked young for a 13-year-old boy. His voice had not yet broken, and he had the innocent confidence of a boy of ten, with wide big brown eyes and long black eyelashes.

"Tell your Uncle Rinaldo what your father is like. Uncle Rinaldo says that your father does not care about us."

"He does!" Diego shot back. His eyes quickly scanned over to the bread and chocolate-hazelnut spread. "Mama, may I?"

"Of course," Sofia said, softening and giving him a little cuddle. "Now sit down, my lovely boy, and tell us about your father." She began to spread three pieces of bread. "I'll make you some sweet tea, too, love."

Rinaldo looked at Diego. "I did not say your father does not care about you."

"Yes, you did," said Sofia. "Or at least you implied it."

"My father is wonderful," Diego said. "Much better than you. You work in a field. He owns the field. He is rich and buys me lots of treats and clothes, and he will buy me a car very soon," he said. "He cannot come and live with us because he lives with an evil witch called Chiari." The young boy said the name like it was some kind of infectious disease. "But one day he will defeat her, and come and live with us forever and ever."

Rinaldo sighed and stared out the window, absentmindedly munching on his bread. "Is that a fact?"

"Yes," Diego said with conviction.

Sofia got up to put the kettle on the stove. "Uncle Rinaldo says your father is lying."

Diego thumped Rinaldo on his arm. "He is not lying!"

"Don't do that, Diego," Sofia said, but in a rather lackluster tone. When she turned away to fix the kettle, she had a small smile on her face.

"You are the liar!" Diego shouted at Rinaldo. "You are just jealous of him. Jealous of us. Everybody is jealous of us." He stuffed a large piece of bread in his mouth and spoke through it. "My father is a hero. You are a... big fat zero."

Rinaldo sighed. He couldn't work up anger for the child. Obviously Bruno, in his deceit, and Sofia, in her utter stupidity, had poisoned his mind. "Well, fine then," he said, getting up. "I will go out for a while. To look for work."

"Yes, go," Sofia said. "And don't think you can still sleep here if you have terrible things to say about Bruno. I don't care if you sleep on the street, if that's your attitude. Fix your mouth before you come back. Bruno is the love of my life and that is that."

Rinaldo shrugged as he walked out of the house and closed the front door behind him.

CHAPTER FOUR

Luigi's vineyards and sprawling castle were on the way to Deborah's, where Kat and Blaine were staying.

"I am honored to ask you to have dinner at my home tonigt," Luigi said from his seat behind the wheel of the Maybach.

"Thank you," Blaine said.

Kat smiled. "We'd love to."

"We'll stop first at Luigi's, and then we'll head over to my place," Deborah said, turning around in her seat to look back at them. Kat just loved the way her eyes sparkled and danced. She was so glad to see her friend truly happy. "I want you to get unpacked and see the house before it gets dark. And my own vineyard. It's a baby vineyard, compared to Luigi's."

The afternoon sun laid a golden veneer over the Italian countryside. The sky was deepening into a lilac color as the sun began to set. The green of the vineyards became lusher and richer in the changing light.

"These are my vineyards," Luigi said. "Well, the Giordano vineyards, to be more precise. They will pass to my sons when I die." He laughed and said, "Hopefully I've got a few good years left."

"I should hope so!" Deborah said, "After all, you're only fifty-five.

"How many sons do you have?" Kat asked.

"Two," Luigi said.

"They're wonderful young men," Deborah said. "They both work in Florence. Leo's a financial analyst, and Matteo's a lawyer. They come down and see Luigi quite regularly."

Luigi laughed. "By the time I'm gone, I'm hoping they'll have cultivated some kind of vague interest in wine, although I'm afraid there's not an inkling of it so far. As it stands now, my vineyards will go to seed under their care."

The vineyards, which stretched out before them as they drove, seemed to be never-ending.

"Are all these yours?" Kat asked.

Luigi laughed and said, "I'm afraid so."

"The castle is the real jewel in the crown," said Deborah. "Wait until you see it, Kat." Kat knew Deborah wasn't boasting. She was just enjoying the dream that her life had become since she'd had the courage to pack up her things in Lindsay, Kansas, and venture half way around the world to start a new life. She wanted to share her joy with Kat, and Kat was touched by it.

"Oh, but it is a nightmare to clean," Luigi said modestly. "My mother, God bless her soul, if she were still alive, would be on her hands and knees day and night scrubbing the place. Unfortunately, I do not have her stamina, and have had to bring in some help."

"Look, look, it's coming up!" Deborah said, clapping her hands with excitement, and turning back to look at Kat and Blaine to see their reaction.

They rounded a bend in the huge Maybach, and...

"Wow!" Kat exclaimed.

The castle, nestled as it was in the Italian countryside and surrounded by lush green vineyards, looked like some sort of a famous landscape painting. *Or perhaps,* Kat thought, *a backdrop on a movie set or theater.* In the early evening sunset, it had a dreamy quality that made it look ethereal. If you blinked your eyes, it might disappear, like something out of a fairytale.

It was a vast stone building, rising up and away from the vines of the vineyards and the terraced lawns that surrounded it. It would have looked like quite an austere stone fortress, if it weren't for two things – one, the soft brown color of the stones, and two, the abundance of greenery in the adjoining grounds. Trees stood all around, and vines and climbers crept all over the castle's face, until it looked quite soft and welcoming.

"That's really something," Blaine said.

"It sure is," Kat said. "It must be like living in a storybook."

"For a while," Luigi said. "Then it becomes normal, like most other things in life."

His statement sounded quite profound, but Kat wasn't sure what to make of it. "What do you mean, Luigi?" she asked.

"I came from a poor family, Ms. Denham. I was determined to make my way out of a life where we had holes in our shoes and some days we had no food for dinner. But I found out money was not everything."

Blaine nodded. "I've come to a similar realization about that," he said. "What made you realize it?"

"Well, as a young boy I got a job carrying farm produce from our small rural village into town for market," Luigi said. "Soon I traded in the market myself, and before long I was doing much bigger deals. I was very afraid of being poor, and all I could think about was money and how to make more and more of it. But what I have come to realize is money can prevent you from suffering from poverty, but it cannot prevent you from suffering from many other things. A broken heart is one of these things."

"Very true," Kat said.

"The mother of my boys, my late wife, died when my boys were nine and seven. I had not paid nearly enough attention to them. I realized this when, after she died, I was faced with raising two young children who were almost strangers to me. I could not even remember their birthdays. All I had done was work and work and work. I measured the success of each day by how much money I had made that day. I kept detailed records of how much I made every day. I had not taken one moment to slow down and cherish what I had."

The atmosphere in the car had changed. It was deep and somber, but not uncomfortable.

"Unfortunately, it was too late for me to reconnect with my wife," Luigi said. "But I put my heart and soul into raising my sons."

"Thank goodness," Deborah said. "They really needed you. And now you have a great relationship with both of them."

Luigi smiled. "Yes, thank God. I feel I am seeing the fruits of my labor. Both my boys are doing well, and are happy with their partners. And I..." He breathed out as he looked across at Deborah. "And I... was blessed with a rare American flower, who happened to bloom in Florence."

Sitting in the back seat with Blaine, Kat looked at him with a sentimental smile and squeezed his hand. Luigi's open, romantic ways were really quite refreshing.

They drove past the castle and traveled on in silence for a while until they arrived in a suburban neighborhood with large modern homes. They turned right onto a tree-lined avenue, then drove a short way down it.

"Here we are," Deborah said. "Home sweet home."

"Oh, is this your house?" Kat asked. "It's lovely!"

"Thanks," Deborah said with a smile.

It really was lovely. It was an intriguing mix between classical Italian architecture and the modern glass and polished steel look that was so popular these days.

There was a rounded portico in the center, set in front of the double front doors, with gleaming rounded steps leading up to the doors, and equally gleaming pillars holding it all in place. Then the building jutted out at each side in orderly right angles. Floor to ceiling glass windows were positioned on each side of the doors, and now that it was just beginning to get a little dark, the golden lights inside the house illuminated the interior and made the whole place look magical. The house was painted white and its flat roof had sleek detailing where it met the walls, making the whole thing look smooth and modern.

"Aww, Primo!" Deborah said as she got out of the car.

A huge dark brown dog came bounding up to her. It had a black muzzle and looked so intimidating that Kat thought twice about getting out of the car. "Whoa, Deborah, that's quite a dog."

Deborah laughed. "He won't bite or anything. He's got a very good sense of who's a good person and who's here to make trouble. He'll be absolutely fine with you." She looked back at Kat's nervous face. "Still, I'll hold his collar."

Blaine was already out of the car, and Kat decided she'd take her chances. She wasn't usually afraid of dogs, in fact, she loved them. Her own two dogs, Jazz and Rudy, brought great joy to her life, but she'd also had some bad experiences with other dogs in the past. "I don't recognize the breed," she said to Deborah. "What is he?"

"A cane corso," Deborah said. "He's an ancestor of the Neapolitan Mastiff."

"Okay," Kat said. "I'm unfamiliar with the breed."

"They're great guard dogs," Luigi said, hauling their suitcases out of the trunk.

"I got him from the family that sold me the house," Deborah said. "They couldn't take him with them when they moved. Thankfully he warmed up to me quickly. He's really a wonderful dog."

"You always wanted a dog, didn't you?" Kat said.

"Yes, but my ex-husband was allergic to them," Deborah said with a laugh. "I should have gotten rid of him a long time ago and had a dog instead. Would have been better company." Everyone laughed.

Primo edged toward Kat, looking at her with suspicion.

"I'll pet him once he gets used to me," Kat said nervously. "And not a moment before."

Deborah laughed as they walked up to the front door. "If he can scare you, Kat, he can scare anybody."

"That's true enough," Luigi said. "I've been hearing all about your detective exploits, Kat."

"And worrying me sick," Blaine said, while nudging Kat and giving her a quick smile. "I feel like I must be married to the bravest woman in the world."

"I'm sure you do," Deborah said. "You're one of a kind, Kat Denham." Then she put the key in the front door and opened it.

The entrance to Deborah's house was truly gorgeous. The house was large with four bedrooms, but by no means a mansion on the scale of Luigi's castle. Still, it had a two-story entrance hall with an elaborate glass skylight and a curved white staircase that led to the upper floor.

"My, my, my!" Kat said. "Look how we're living it up!"

Deborah blushed. "Oh, stop. Italians just like a little grandeur, is all."

"Such interesting architecture," Blaine said, looking around. There were quite a few curved surfaces and walls, including an unusual design where all the rooms led into the hallway, with their own curved entrance spaces. "What a unique home."

"Thank you," Deborah said. "I think my favorite thing about it is the high ceilings."

"I just love how you've decorated it," Kat said. Almost everything was white with bronze and gold accents. The dark heavy wooden doors contrasted beautifully with the color scheme. There was some elaborate white plasterwork at the top of various pillars, which added a more classical Italian flair, but overall the house had a very clean, modern feel to it. The floor was marble, with decorative circular patterns with tiny flashes of gold, bronze, orange, and turquoise at each doorway.

"I actually didn't do any of the decorating," Deborah said. "Not even the furniture. It was all included when I bought the house. The prior owners moved to England to renovate a large country manor, and they said this sort of furniture would stand out like a sore thumb in their new home. They were going to go 'antiquing', as they called it, to buy furniture. Now please follow me, and I'll take you to your room."

Kat and Blaine were delighted with the guestroom Deborah led them to. Not only did it have a wonderfully luxurious four-poster bed, it had thick cream colored rugs, a two-person jacuzzi tub in the gleaming bathroom, and a large balcony overlooking the back garden.

"Oh, Deborah!" Kat said as they all stepped onto the balcony. "You're spoiling us."

Deborah gave her a quick side-hug and a grin. "Glad to be able to. After all, you saved my life, so it's the least I can do," she said referring to when the coed's murderer had threatened to take Kat and Deborah's lives before Deborah had left Lindsay for Italy.

Blaine rested his hands on the railing and looked out over the garden. "This outdoor space you have is just beautiful."

"Thanks," Deborah said. "I have some fruit trees, and I'm starting a vegetable garden. That's in addition to the vineyard which is located towards the back of the property. I'm thinking of what else I should do. Perhaps a little swimming pool, or an ornamental pond. I'm considering a number of possibilities. That is… if I'm going to be staying here for long. Who knows?" She smiled at Luigi, her eyes full of light and love. "Now, who's hungry? Let's head over to Luigi's and have dinner."

CHAPTER FIVE

Chiari Lombardi was a master at hiding her emotions. She wasn't born that way, it was a skill she'd learned over the years she'd been with Bruno.

It all started on her wedding night. Her family was from Lazio, the district on the Italian mainland where they were prominent members of society. Her parents had moved to Sardinia for business purposes, and she and her much younger brothers and sisters were the first generation of the family to be born in Sardinia, and as such, much was expected of them. The family had quite a fearsome reputation in Lazio for getting the best of the best, and stopping at nothing to get it. Everyone's eyes were firmly locked on the new Sardinian branch of the family. There was an unspoken warning always hanging in the air: *Don't let the Romano family down.*

So she had done what she was meant to do – find a handsome, wealthy young suitor to marry. At first she'd been in love with Salvatore, but she'd been quickly talked out of that match by both the Romano and the Lombardi family. His head was full of dreams, they said. He wanted to be a politician so he could help disadvantaged people, an idea which seemed utterly idealistic and even childish to them. Chiari had thought it was romantic, but she'd quickly been set straight by her elders and by Bruno.

Bruno had filled every box on her family's checklist. Rich.

Forward (some would even say aggressive). Confident. Well-bred. Ambitious. He fit in better with Chiari's family than she did herself. She, with her sensitive heart and dreams of making the world a better place, had always felt like somewhat of an outcast. Her family clearly thought there was something slightly wrong with her, although they never quite said as much, but when Bruno was around, they embraced her. They kept saying things like, "You're making the Romanos so very proud," and her hungry heart lapped it all up.

On the day of her wedding, the family beamed and clapped as she was escorted down the aisle by her father, but that night, when Bruno had become angry when she had mentioned Salvatore's name.

He was drunk from far too much wedding wine. In their wedding suite at one of Sardinia's most prestigious hotels, she said it was a shame Salvatore had not been able to attend the wedding. Bruno hit the roof, called her all sorts of disgusting names, and said that if she ever mentioned Salvatore's name again, she would have a bruise or a scar to remember the incident by.

It was then, with her heart feeling like it was breaking inside her chest, that Chiari realized she had trapped herself in a cage. But life with Bruno hadn't turned out to be all bad. In fact, he could often be absolutely charming, especially when he was happy. He went all out and bought her many gifts. Not just expensive ones, but thoughtful ones, that showed he really knew her taste and cared for her. He let her spend money however she pleased, and never once berated her about it.

They tried to have a child for many years. Chiari had always imagined herself being a mother with umpteen little ones running around her feet. Her own mother had been quite cold, which had always made Chiari feel alone, but Chiari's aching heart had all the love in the world to give. But it wasn't to be. After a raft of tests, and hundreds and thousands of dollars spent on every treatment under the sun, her doctor finally said, "It's just not going to happen, Mrs. Lombardi."

After she'd heard the sad pronouncement by her doctor, Chiari had mourned terribly. She'd written baby name lists in the back of her diaries since she was about eleven years old. Long ago she'd decided on Diego Domenico for a boy and Vittoria Noemi for a girl.

Throughout all that, Bruno had shown that he did indeed have a good side. He was patient and calm and kind. Chiari knew that many men, especially rich successful men with estates to pass on to the next generation, would have been very disappointed that she couldn't bear him a son. Maybe even angry, but if he was frustrated, he'd never let on.

But still, at other times, Bruno could have rages. It was in these moments she learned that crying would not help stop the rages. The only thing that would work was turning off her emotions like a tap, sitting with a face like stone, and only bringing her spirit back out from its hiding place once his rage had passed. It was a great skill to have, and now that she'd found out his dirty secret, she was employing it during every moment of the day and night.

Chiari had no one to talk to. Sometimes, when her heart swelled with pain in light of the betrayal, she turned to the saints. She clutched her pink glass rosary praying the rosary until she could barely talk, then prayed over her statues in the little altar room she'd set up. Other times, she just collapsed on the bed and cried, feeling so wretched she was sure the divine wouldn't possibly listen to her.

Today was one of the latter days. It was a blazing hot afternoon outside. She was lying on top of the comforter on her and Bruno's bed, feeling nothing at all. She was more than numb, she was an empty shell. Today, she couldn't even cry. Her mind took her back to thirteen years ago. She could remember it all, clear as day.

"Sofia," Chiari had said, on the brink of tears. "I'll miss you so much."

Sofia Ossani, their maid, sat on the couch, her blonde hair tied back in a neat chignon. She was always immaculately well-groomed, which Chiari had liked. She thought maybe they had something in common, since Chiari always had her nails, hair, and makeup done. It almost felt like some kind of armor. A psychological armor against the difficulties in life.

Sofia and Chiari hugged each other tightly, and Sofia tucked some of Chiari's dark hair behind her ear. "You are a good woman," Sofia had said. "Be strong and keep praying, and you will be happy."

Chiari had confided everything to her, about her marriage, about how unhappy she sometimes was in the gilded cage in which she lived, and even about Salvatore. She had never told a soul before, but there was something about Sofia that was so warm and kind that she felt like Mother Earth to Chiari, and the whole thing just came spilling out of her mouth one day.

Since then they had been like kindred souls, though Sofia was certainly the 'leader' of the two, always giving Chiari little pep talks. "Men are not worth all that much," she had always said. "Especially not your tears."

When Sofia became pregnant and the father didn't want anything to do with her or the child, she stuck by her word. Chiari was horrified, and cried on her behalf, but Sofia stuck her chin in the air and smiled. "I will not cry over this. Sofia Ossani cannot be broken." She declared that she would move to the other end of the island and start a new life.

"But how will you survive?" Chiari had asked, her heart beating with worry for her friend.

Sofia had pinched her gently under the chin, like someone would a child. "Don't you worry about Sofia. I will get by."

But Chiari couldn't help herself from worrying. The thought of her friend suffering and struggling to feed her child kept her awake at night. She woke Bruno up one night and explained the situation to him. "Can we help?" she'd asked. "Just give her some money for a few months to help her get started?"

"If you want," he said in a disapproving tone of voice. "Though you should not get so involved with her. She is only a servant."

"Not a servant, Bruno!" Chiari said passionately. "She's a person!"

"Yeah, yeah," Bruno said. Then he rolled over and soon started snoring.

Chiari set her plan in motion, so that by the time Sofia was scheduled to leave, she had everything in place. She handed Sofia a huge bunch of flowers, a box that contained a very expensive necklace (it was her own and she loved it, but she thought Sofia might love it even more) and an envelope thick with cash.

Sofia and Chiari cried into each other's arms as they hugged. Then Chiari rubbed Sofia's belly and said, "Love you, little one. Maybe someday you will meet Auntie Chiari."

But Sofia had never returned. Never written. Never even called.

And only now, thirteen years later, did Chiari know why: *Because the child in Sofia's belly was Bruno's.*

Only now he was a thirteen-year-old boy. An angry thirteen-year-old boy who had been consistently lied to, Chiari deduced from the letter she'd received from him.

It was written in an angry scrawl...

To Chiari Lombardi

You are a devil woman. Leave Bruno, my father, alone so he can come back to his family and stay with us forever. No one knows I am writing this, but I am not afraid of you like everyone else is. Let my father go. NOW.

Diego Ossani-Lombardi

Chiari's world had closed in on her when she'd read the letter for the first time. Thankfully there had been a couch nearby, so when her legs gave out, she was able to stagger over to it and collapse without hurting herself.

She'd tucked the letter into her pocket and since then seemingly read it a million times. The paper the letter had been written on was well worn now. The word that stabbed her through the heart like a knife was 'Diego,' the name she'd picked out for her son years ago, and confided to both Sofia and Bruno. It was the cherry on top of the icing of betrayal. She didn't know who had hurt her more, or what had hurt her more.

Even now, as she lay on the bed, so motionless she felt dead, she was confused. Did she care that Bruno would likely bring this 'false Diego' to their home, and give him everything? Of course, Bruno's son, regardless of who his mother was, would inherit the winery and everything else. What if Bruno died before she did? She would probably be kicked out of her house and home, while Sofia would be moved in by little Diego and become the new queen of the Lombardi kingdom.

It wasn't the money. Although Chiari had become accustomed to a very high standard of luxury living over the years, this went deeper than that. Much deeper. Beyond the betrayal, it was about her identity. Though the 'not good enough' feeling her family had given her still lingered under the surface of her life, she'd managed to mask it very, very well. She was the successful, beautiful, honorable woman of the Lombardi empire, the Lombardi Empress, so to speak, and that position allowed her a safe place to hide all her insecurities. It kept her family happy, too.

But if Diego was brought in, everyone would know, she thought. The shame of it all would come back full circle onto her.

I was not enough to hold Bruno Lombardi.
I was not able to give him a child.
Bruno chose a maid to procreate with, over me!
I have lost power to a thirteen-year-old boy and a maid!

Chiari lay staring at the ceiling. Her life had come to a standstill. Every moment dragged out, seeming like an eternity. She couldn't possibly confront Bruno. She'd stand to lose everything. She'd have to admit it was all reality, too. Despite Bruno's difficult moments, she loved him. She was deeply fond of him. They'd had nearly twenty years together. Another reason she couldn't confront him was she was afraid of her own rage.

She'd learned to tightly control any anger she'd felt ever since her wedding night. She didn't dare get angry with Bruno, so once again, she tried to control it, even though her fury was so heavy it felt like a lead weight around her neck.

Chiari's life seemed to be crashing down, piling up as rubble and ruins around her ankles. She hadn't chosen this. But now, for reasons she had no part in or control over, she was forced to bear the burden.

CHAPTER SIX

Salvatore Lombardi sat at Gianna's Beach Bar, as he did most days, and drowned his sorrows. Gianna herself handed him his whiskey on the rocks and didn't make eye contact. He knew why. He had a tendency to overshare, and overshare the same things repeatedly at that, but he was too miserable to care. She might have thought it was annoying to have the same story repeated to her, but for him, it was torture, having the same tragedy played over and over again in his head, each and every miserable day of his life.

He'd had plenty of advice from Gianna's patrons over the years.

"Forget about them. Live your life."

"Get therapy if you have to."

"Man up."

But nothing got through.

He was at least business savvy enough not to drone on and on about it to his own Bed & Breakfast guests. He knew that he'd struck the jackpot by somehow managing to get them into this old rundown town, and he had Alessa to thank for that. He'd hired her to do a bit of cleaning, but she'd quickly proven herself to be ambitious and hardworking and, in all fairness, somewhat of a visionary. She kept saying, "Oh, but that would look nice in green," or "We really need some flowers right here."

So he'd given her a little money here and there to buy paint and cushions and curtains and whatever else she said would brighten up the place, and she'd transformed the whole B and B into something quite new and fresh looking.

She'd also uploaded photographs of the rooms onto Booking and TripAdvisor, and now they had people coming in from all over the world Visitors generally rated the area as poor, but the B and B as excellent. Alessa was even trying to fix that discrepancy, though, and had started to think about creating cultural tours to show off the hidden gems in the community. Salvatore thought Alessa was the only hidden gem in the community. He'd lost all interest in the business and often thought he might give the business to Alessa, but he never got as far as planning it out in any real detail.

Instead, he ended up at the bar, drinking.

How different life could have been...

No matter how he tried to distract himself, this 'different life' was always where his mind ended up. It was almost impossible to believe where he was when he walked the alleys of the slow, ramshackle seaside town, with mangy stray dogs begging and young boys falling over themselves to sell some poorly-made handcraft to the tourists who had lost their way.

He hadn't made any friends here. How could he, when they lived here too? When they were living in the present, accepting this reality as their lives? Rather, each day he just talked out his story to anyone who would listen. Sometimes it was a local who hadn't been around for a while. Sometimes it was the people who lived up on the mountain and came down for flour and sugar now and again. Sometimes it was a tourist. Or a fisherman. Or on really bad days, one of the mangy dogs.

Today, it was a young Australian tourist. A bronzed woman in her

20's with scruffy clothes, a camera around her neck, and a seemingly fearless attitude. She had walked into Gianna's bar and ordered herself three beers – they were on special.

"So where are you from, then?" Salvatore asked in thick English.

"Australia," the woman said. "You?"

Salvatore smiled. This was his standard opening. It could get them into the conversation faster. "From one of the finest places in Sardinia. The Lombardi wine estate. You know of it?"

The woman shrugged, looking distinctly unimpressed. "I'm not really into wine and all that. I'm here to see life, real life. And capture it on film. I'm a photographer."

Salvatore laughed. "Oh, you won't see any real life around here. This is the land that time forgot."

"You're disillusioned," the woman said directly.

"You bet I am. You would be, too, if you had lived the life I have."

"Can I take your picture?" she said, already sliding off her barstool.

Salvatore was beginning to get annoyed. "No."

"Aww, come on. I'll pay you."

"I don't want your money!" Salvatore snapped. "Just because you see me here in this disgusting place with these clothes, don't think I'm just like the rest of the people who live here. I wasn't born here. This isn't me. It's just what has happened to me, where desperation has brought me."

The Australian nodded thoughtfully. "So this is your last resort? Ooh, I like that for a blog post title. The Last Resort."

"For a what title?"

"Nothing," the woman said quickly. She got back on her barstool. "I'd love to hear your story. Can I include it in my blog?"

"You can include it in whatever you like," Salvatore snapped. He felt pressure building in his chest, the same pressure that built every day. He felt it would burst if he didn't get his story out, and fast. "I was in love…"

"Wait. I'm Blair. What's your name?"

"People call me Sal."

"You have an interesting face for photography, Sal. Your nose is… well, you'll make a fascinating profile."

"My nose was broken in a bar fight. Now, did you come to ask me about my nose or my story?"

"Go ahead," Blair said.

"Right. I was in love. And rightly so. Anyone with half a mind would be in love with this woman. Chiari Romano was a goddess somehow mistakenly put on earth by our Creator. You should have seen how her eyes danced, like a thousand candles at mass flickering in a gentle breeze."

Given that he'd told this story thousands of times before, he had come up with what he thought were rather poetic phrases. "Her smile was like the most beautiful sunset you'd ever see. I thought about her every waking moment. How could I not?"

"How long ago was this?" asked Blair.

"Many years. It goes back into the mists of time," Salvatore said. "You see?" he blurted out, both soothed and angered by what he felt was the heartbreaking poetry in his own speech. "You see I am not from here? My spirit and culture are from somewhere entirely different. I was not born here, among the spit and the cockroaches."

"A dramatic fall from wealth?" Blair said, looking excited. She was looking for a story as much as Salvatore wanted to tell one.

"Not a fall. I was pushed! I had proposed to Chiari before I left for college. Under a blanket of stars we lay, atop a hill. I asked if she would do me the honor of being my special princess for eternity. She said she would. We agreed that once college was finished, we would be together and officially marry."

He took a long swig of his whiskey. His heart still ached in his chest when he told this part of the story. Sometimes the fury leaped up afterward, sometimes it did not. He was not sure if it would today. It seemed the story had a will of its own, gripping his heart and twisting it in whichever direction it wanted to go on any given day.

"So what happened then?" Blair asked as she motioned to Gianna and said, "Bring him another whiskey, please." Then she took a swig from her beer.

"My father died while I was in my final year of college."

"Oh, I'm so sorry," Blair said. "My father died when…"

"Don't be!" Salvatore spat. "He was a cruel, vindictive man right up until the end. He pretended like he was a good man, spoiling my brother Bruno and taking him under his wing. But really, he was a squirming mass of maggots underneath the surface. An evil man to my mother, God rest her soul. She deserved much better. And a bully to me. I was a child, and I could not defend myself, as much as I tried." He took a sip of whiskey from the fresh glass.

"My father, in his signature style, left our entire award-winning vineyard and mansion to Bruno, along with most of his fortune. I inherited a pittance. Just a few pennies. Everyone said it was because Bruno was the eldest, but I knew better. It was because he hated me."

"Wow, so you were really rich before all that, huh?" Blair looked far too excited. "Then this is a real fall from grace."

"The worst is yet to come," Salvatore said. "While I was away, my father and Bruno had poisoned Chiari's mind against me. They told her all sorts of lies. They said I had another girlfriend at the university. In fact, I had girls everywhere, according to them. Also, they told her I was going nowhere. I was a lazy waster. In fact, I was at college studying political science because I wanted to help people. I wanted to make people's lives better.

"I had considered being a doctor, but I thought a politician would be better. Perhaps I could protect people from the mafia. Perhaps I could feed the hungry." Salvatore laughed bitterly. "What a stupid young dreamer I was. I envisioned Chiari and me living happily with our children, while I changed the world." He looked Blair up and down. "I hope you are not so stupid."

Blair held her hands up. "I don't believe in politics. I think all politicians are liars."

"Before I knew what had happened, my father had suggested that Bruno and Chiari marry each other instead of her marrying me. 'You have the wrong brother' they said to her, and all of them thought it was very funny. I did not attend the wedding. I would have fallen down dead on the spot.

"Instead, I accepted my father's pittance and came out here to this godforsaken place. I bought a B and B and tried to do my best. But my empty bedroom haunted me. When I walked the streets, I thought every dark-haired woman who passed me was Chiari. I could not look into another woman's eyes without wishing they were hers."

Blair blew a stream of air out of her lips. "Whoa. This is some heavy stuff."

"Life is heavy, young lady, and the sooner you get to know it the better. Many people find that out as they get older and tragedy strikes. They live a blissful lie beforehand. For others of us, we see the tragedy clearly from an early age."

"I'm not sure I agree," Blair said. "Sure, bad stuff happens. But good stuff happens, too. There's a lot of awesome stuff in the world."

Salvatore smiled at her, the first time he'd smiled in a long time. "The innocence of youth."

"Don't patronize me," Blair said. "Seriously. You could change your life. Okay, so you're not Brad Pitt, but you're not a bad looking man. You could go out there and get yourself a loving wife."

"No one would be Chiari," Salvatore said.

"No, but… wow. You're really in love with this woman, huh?"

Salvatore felt his eyes glaze over with tears. "Yes. And if she was happy, I would have let her go. But the truth is, my brother never loved her. I knew that. She was just a trophy to him, because she was so beautiful. And because he had stolen her from me."

Blair nodded, drinking it all in.

"And news comes down here from time to time. His business success carries far, because of his public persona. My brother has a mistress. Even with a child. How dare he do that to Chiari? She deserves the best. It would not surprise me if he is loose with his insults and his fists with her, too, just like my father was with my mother."

He swallowed down tears and rage. "I cannot let this happen!" Then his voice softened. "But I cannot 'take' Chiari, because she is not an object. She is a person with her own thoughts and feelings. With her own choice… I just do not see why she has made this choice, this choice that causes her untold misery."

Blair looked at Salvatore with a burning intensity in her eyes. "Perhaps it's not over. Perhaps there is a way you can get her back. Maybe she is waiting for you to rescue her."

Salvatore sat up straight. Blair had gotten his attention. No one had ever said or suggested such a thing. Usually, by this point in the story, their eyes had glazed over, and they stammered out any excuse they could think of to get away.

"I don't know," Salvatore said. "I doubt it."

"Maybe, maybe not," Blair agreed. "But Sal, anyone can tell you're a great guy. Don't throw your life away regretting the past. You could have a future, too." Blair gave him a firm pat on the back. "How about that picture now? It's not going to be so gloomy, would be my guess. I'll change the whole spin of my blog post. Make it like you're going to move on up. Getting your story out for the first time must have really helped, huh? Guess you're glad you bumped into me?"

Blair stepped back a few paces to snap the picture, and Salvatore actually managed a smile.

CHAPTER SEVEN

The drive to Luigi's castle took them all, Luigi, Deborah, Kat, and Blaine, through acres and acres of vineyards, up a long winding driveway, and finally onto a large, circular, gravel area with a large fountain in the center and trees all around.

The castle itself was even more exquisite when viewed close up. Some of the vines coursing across the face of it were flowering, gorgeous fuchsias in royal purples and pure whites. The castle looked even larger from close up. Kat tried to count the number of windows going across the top floor, but lost her place when she got to eighteen.

"This is incredible," Blaine said. "Truly exquisite."

"It is, isn't it?" Kat gushed. "Is there time for a tour before dinner? Not of the whole place, that would probably take hours and hours, but just the main rooms?"

"Of course," Luigi said, parking the Maybach. "Mrs. Bianchi has prepared our dinner to be ready at 7:00 p.m., so we have a little time. Let's go around to the back first."

"You'll both love it," Deborah said.

And they did.

It took a while to get around to the back, since the castle was so wide. They passed little herb gardens, well-tended bushes bearing all kinds of flowers, olive trees, and a little water garden with a trickling man-made stream bubbling over a gorgeous rock formation.

"I dedicated this garden to my father," Luigi said, then he laughed. "When I was a child, he always liked to sit by a stream when he felt stressed out. And his stress was probably caused by me. It was infrequent that he took me with him to visit a nearby stream, but when he did, those were some of the best moments of my childhood."

They finally reached the back of the castle, and Deborah hadn't been lying, it certainly didn't disappoint. There was a sweeping veranda which ran the entire length of the back side of the castle. It was designed in a grand, almost royal-looking style, with vast stone steps leading up to it.

Kat climbed the steps behind the others, looking around in awe. As they got further and further up, the awe only increased. The view was incredible. It was so incredible it didn't even look real. It was more like a painting than real life. It made Kat feel almost philosophical about just how large the world was. She was transported out of her mind, and into something else entirely. She saw cars weaving through the countryside in the distance, and spotted little country houses dotted here and there.

The others were silent for a moment, also swept away by the view.

"I come here when I need to be reminded that my problems are small," Luigi said with a laugh. "That there is more to life than the wine business."

"It's like the house of a statesman," Blaine said. "I could imagine this would be a great place to think about world problems, or at least the local community. After all, you can see all of the community in front of you."

Everyone laughed.

"Actually, you're right. It was my grandfather's, and he was a statesman. The castle had been in the family for many generations."

Luigi led the way inside. Opening onto the veranda, there were numerous floor to ceiling double doors. Only one was open, and long curtains fluttered by the open window. Luigi pulled them aside for everyone else to step through.

Kat suppressed a gasp as they walked in. It was some kind of a reception room, though she wondered what the Italians called it. A living room sounded far too small. A salon? A parlor? A smoking room?

It was like stepping right into the past, complete with bigger-than-life size portraits on the walls in gilded golden frames. Enormous chandeliers hung overhead, while ancient rugs graced the polished floor. It was all very intricate and detailed, and everywhere Kat looked there was some kind of decoration or ornament that looked like a very expensive antique.

Luigi continued his story, "But my grandfather lost everything when one of the mafias set their sights on him. He tried to stand up to them, but needless to say, it went extremely badly. He went from a successful, happily married man who was full of joy and love which spread through his political influence, to a homeless, divorced alcoholic, who had nothing pleasant to say about anybody or to anybody.

"The couple of times I met him I was terrified of him. I remember he and my father having a fight, an actual physical fight, when I was about six. We cut contact with him after that. As a child, he was the stuff of nightmares, but as I got older and listened to more and more of my father's stories, I realized that really, the man was not evil. He was just broken, so broken he couldn't put himself back together.

"And it broke my father, too, who also turned to the bottle. So... when I saw that the castle was on the market... the mafia who had seized it had been driven away when their leader was killed by rivals and the locals started fighting more strongly against them – it roused something within me. Like, maybe I could put everything right by buying it. I know it sounds silly, rather superstitious, but I think it has worked. Ever since I bought it, life has been good. My father passed away just after I purchased it, as if I'd brought him some kind of peace."

The more he spoke, the better Kat liked Luigi. He was such a warm-hearted man, and she was so glad Deborah had found someone like him. Kat was sure he'd be kind to her and protect her from any kind of harm.

"I'm sure your grandfather would be proud of you," Blaine said. "Did the antiques come with the house? Were they family antiques?"

"No," Luigi said. "Well, yes, some of them were. The mafia had gutted the castle of anything of value and sold it off. They'd even pulled out some of the plasterwork and structural elements, which I had to rebuild. Local powers took control of the property when they managed to drive the mafia out, but they couldn't afford the upkeep on it. I had to do a lot of structural repair work. Then I hired a couple of antique scouts.

"My best find was this…" He pointed to a portrait. "That is my great-grandfather. We tracked that down to a private collection in Hong Kong, of all places. Those mafia really have connections." Luigi laughed. "Anyway, shall we continue?"

He led them through a series of similarly grand rooms. Kat particularly liked one that had a blue and gold color scheme. It looked like a place where a king and queen would live. "Queen Deborah," she teased as she looked at her friend.

Deborah laughed. "I'm just glad Luigi has Mrs. Bianchi and her team. Can you imagine how much cleaning we'd have to do, just the two of us?"

Kat chuckled. "You'd be dusting all day and all night."

"It's nearly 7:00 p.m. now," Luigi said, looking at his watch. "Let's go to the wine room."

When they were back in the grand hallway, he opened a large wooden door that led downstairs into a charming space. It had rustic stone walls, but paired with a modern shiny black tiled floor, it was a perfect mix between old and new. The lights were dimmed, and the set table flickered with soft candlelight.

"Sometimes Luigi rents out this space for events," Deborah said.

"I can see why. It's beautiful," Kat said.

The walls were covered with wine racks in enclosed glass cases.

"Great presentation of the wines," Blaine complimented Luigi.

"Thank you," Luigi said, smiling proudly, as if the wine bottles were his children. "Each case has a different temperature, so each bottle is in its own ideal habitat, so to speak."

"Brilliant idea," said Kat.

"Now, let's eat!" Luigi said, leading them to the table. The appetizers were ready on platters and wine bottles had been placed on the white tablecloth. "Wow, Mrs. Bianchi has done a wonderful job."

"You said you hold events here?" Kat said. "Will yours be the first wedding held here?"

"No, it won't," Luigi said with a smile. "I've been glad to host many of them here. My grandfather was always a family man, so this brings me great joy. I think we may be around the 100th couple to tie the knot here."

"And it's going to be a big wedding," Deborah said, rolling her eyes. "I told Luigi to try to stick to twenty people."

"But that's not the Italian way," Luigi said with a laugh. "Everyone will say I snubbed them."

Kat laughed. "So how many guests are you expecting?"

Deborah winced. "About two hundred." Then she reached out and squeezed Kat's hand. "I'm so glad you can be here to be my matron of honor. That means the world to me. You can be crowd control, too."

Kat smiled warmly. "We wouldn't have missed it for the world. And I'll bring my cattle prod to control the crowd."

"Who will be your best man, Luigi?" Blaine asked.

"My friend Bruno Lombardi. You've probably heard of Lombardi wines?"

"I certainly have," Kat said.

"Of course," Blaine said. "We have those back home."

Luigi smiled. "He's doing great. We met in Florence many, many years ago when we were both little more than kids, ready to further our careers. He'd come at the behest of his father, to learn more about wine. I was doing the same, reluctantly, only because my father wanted me to. We both shared feelings about our fathers, and then became friends for life."

The next two hours were spent enjoying the special dinner of *torta di Gorgonzola e Pere, Risotto Affumicano con Pistacchi di Paolo, Stemperata di Pollo,* and *Biancomangiare.*

"Luigi, that was delicious," Blaine said with a grin. My compliments to your chef. A tart, risotto, chicken and blancmange. I couldn't have asked for anything more delicious. My stomach also thanks you."

Now that dinner was finished, Kat felt happy and rather sleepy.

She couldn't keep herself from yawning every other minute or so. "Sorry," she said. "I think it's jetlag."

"Perhaps we'll skip the nightcap," said Deborah, "or have it back at my house. Otherwise, I have a feeling Kat will be snoring into her Bailey's."

Kat chuckled. "You're right about that," she just about managed to finish saying before she yawned yet again.

Luigi drove them home, and they arranged to meet again the next day.

"Thank you for everything," Blaine told him as they pulled into Deborah's driveway.

"Don't mention it! Don't mention it," Luigi said, sounding almost offended. He walked Deborah to the door and gave her a kiss. Then he ruffled Primo on the head before leaving.

Primo followed them into the house. Deborah paused and turned around. She wagged her finger at him and said in a funny voice, "Hey, Mr. Primo. Where do you think you're going?"

Primo walked back a little, looking sheepish, and Kat couldn't help but burst out laughing. "Aww, he looks so sweet! Don't you let him inside?"

"It's not really done here," Deborah said. "He was always an outside dog and he seemed quite happy. Lately he's started following me in, though. I'm thinking about changing his routine, but I'm not sure I know enough about dogs to do it successfully. I'm doing a lot of research about it online."

Kat was glad Deborah was taking dog ownership seriously. So many people didn't, and seeing how much Jazz and Rudy depended on her and loved her, it just broke her heart.

Primo came over to her and nudged her. She bent down and

ruffled him under his neck. "How are you doing Primo? You're a lovely boy." She looked up at Deborah. "I love the name."

"I know, right? It's very appropriate, considering he's my first dog," Deborah said, then laughed. "Particularly since he thinks he's number one in this house."

"Bless him," Kat said, then placed her head against his. "Are you the big dog around here? Yes, you are!"

"Don't encourage him," Deborah said with a laugh. "Now I've got to put him back outside and then why don't we have that nightcap?"

CHAPTER EIGHT

Sofia kneeled behind the screen of the confessional and made the sign of the cross. "Bless me, Father, for I have sinned. It has been nearly three years since my last confession. These are my sins."

A long silence stretched out between her and the priest. Sofia felt like she was drowning. But that feeling was no different from what she'd felt during the past few days. It was the reason she was here in the first place. But now it seemed the water was gushing down her throat with great force, and she was about to fall deep down into a watery grave.

"So…"

Her mind tangled itself in knots as she tried to work out where to start.

"Yes?" the priest said gently.

"I have been having an affair with a married man. I thought that… well, I thought it would be excused by God because we were in love, in true love. Our love was the real one. Their marriage was a mistake. A trick of the devil, he has called it. We were the ones who were meant to be together. We're spiritually married. I know God would ordain us to be married, not them."

She so desperately wanted the priest to understand, to agree, to absolve her. But he was silent. She felt panic mount in her chest. All she could do was ramble on, her words tumbling out faster and faster.

"And, well, he told me that they were living in a chaste relationship, like brother and sister. Even when it first began, he told me that. They looked romantic and happy together, but he let me in on a secret – it was all a farce, a front. She had never loved him. She'd loved his brother Salvatore, but switched over to Bruno when she found out he would be the one inheriting all his father's wealth and property. So you see, Father? You see how their marriage is not a true union of love before God?"

The priest said gently, "You are here to confess your own sins. Not those of others."

Sofia let out a little sob. "Yes, Father. So… I had a child by this man. Thirteen years ago. Ever since then he has promised that he would break it off with this false wife of his. He assured me they slept in separate beds, that their marriage has long been over, and they live together like brother and sister. No, in fact, like strangers. All she is interested in is buying expensive things from abroad. He says she does not even pray."

"Again, your own sins, please."

"My only sin has been to be a loving woman, Father. A trusting woman." Her voice caught in her throat. This was the thing she didn't want to say, the thing she didn't want to admit. "But, Father, I am afraid that I have trusted the wrong man." She broke down into a sob, then stayed silent for a long time. It felt like the confession booth was closing in on her – like the whole world was closing in on her.

"Go on," the priest said calmly.

"Maybe my brother was right," she said hollowly, then continued. "The man came to my house to visit, as he so often does." Her voice cracked. "He paid for my house, Father. I thought it was because he was a good man, and he would come to live with us someday, like he always promised. But maybe..." She swallowed her tears. "Well, he came to my home. He likes a particular brand of perfume that I wear, and I had run out. So I ran to the shop to get some. When I returned, I heard him in the bedroom, talking on the phone to Chiari, his devil wife."

She desperately wanted the priest to say something, but he wouldn't. It made her angry. Furious.

"And he was saying to her how much he loves her and cannot wait to return home," she spat. It was the word 'home' that had gotten to her the most. It devalued her and all she had to give. She had been waiting so long for him to come home, the home she shared with Diego, his very own son!

He had always phrased it that way, too. He had always said, "That cold, soulless mansion, with that cold, soulless woman? It is just a mansion to me. It will never be home anymore. She has destroyed it. Home is where the heart is. And my heart is with you." Then he would lean forward and kiss her, and they'd make passionate love.

But had that all been a lie?

"And... he sounded real when he spoke to her. His voice was full of love and affection... the same love and affection he gives to me." She broke down and sobbed uncontrollably. She felt so alone in the world. For so many years she had lived only for Bruno. She had few friends, for the people in the village were so poor she had little in common with any of them.

She was always wary of them trying to get something from her, or come into her beautiful house and steal things. She had once been poor, and wanted to distance herself from poverty as much as possible. After all, she was Bruno Lombardi's future wife, not just some poor village woman. But now... what was she? Had her brother Rinaldo been right? Was she nothing more than Bruno's piece of candy on the side?

"Perhaps he was just faking to her," she said. "Perhaps he has to keep up the pretense." That thought was comforting for only a moment. "But he told me they did not even speak to each other. He told me all they had together was icy silence. But on the phone, that was the furthest thing from icy silence I've ever heard."

She let it all sink in, and felt like she was carrying the weight of the world on her shoulders.

"So now... where do I go? What do I do? What is the truth? I have been praying every day that he will see the light, let loose the reigns of the devil, and come to live in this true marriage, where he will be loved and respected as my husband. Just like God intended..."

"It is a sin to pray for a marriage under God to end," the priest said.

"But is it under God, even if she was just doing it for status and wealth? If she does not truly love him?"

"You do not see what goes on behind closed doors," the priest said. "The marriage is his responsibility under God. If he did not seek an annulment, he has made a commitment to his wife to be with her until death does them part. Do not put yourself on Satan's side and try to tear apart what God has put together."

Sofia felt so confused. The narrative she had told herself, about Satan being the author of Bruno and Chiari's marriage, was crumbling. She had always thought herself on the righteous side, patiently waiting for Bruno to free himself from the shackles Chiari and the devil himself had put on him. But now a horrific thought was stirring within her. Perhaps she was the one who was sinning.

"I don't know, Father. I am confused. I am so, so confused." Her voice broke. "Is it so wrong to want to be with the man I love? With the father of my child? Is it so wrong to want us to live as husband and wife?"

"Yes," the priest said shortly. "You do not need to be confused. Divine law is very clear. You have committed numerous serious sins. You have committed adultery with a married man, and you have allied yourself with Satan to pray for the downfall of their union.

"You will incur eternal punishment. The divine spirit of God in your soul is dying, and you are on the road to hell. You have damaged the Word of God by carrying on with a married man and disrespecting the sacred sacrament of marriage. You have also attempted to use prayer for the work of evil."

Sofia let all the priest had said sink in. She didn't know if she believed it or not. Half of her did, and felt devastated. Her stomach felt like it had dropped to the floor. But as soon as she felt that sensation, an anger arose in her. None of this was fair! None of this was right! What sin had she committed, except to love? Except to trust?

"Are you deeply and truly remorseful for what you have done?" the priest asked.

Sofia tried to bat away the angry part of her, and focus on the guilt twisting in her gut. "Yes, Father," she responded

"Say the act of contrition."

Sofia knew this front to back. She had recited it since she was a child, sometimes with feeling, often just as words coming out of her mouth. "My God, I am sorry for my sins with all my heart. In choosing to do wrong and failing to do good, I have sinned against you whom I should love above all things."

This made her feel angry. "I firmly intend, with your help, to do penance, to sin no more, and to avoid whatever leads me to sin." How could she avoid Bruno, the love of her life? "Our Savior Jesus Christ suffered and died for us. In His name, my God, have mercy. Amen."

The priest then said, "And I absolve you from your sins in the name of the Father, Son, and the Holy Spirit," while Sofia made the sign of the cross over herself and wondered why life was so painful and unfair.

"Give thanks to the Lord, for he is good," the Priest said.

"His mercy endures forever," Sofia parroted.

"Your eternal punishment is now remitted. The temporal punishment must be worked off with penance." He paused for a moment. "Your penance is to pray for the success and blessing of the marriage between this man and his wife every day for the next seven days, and to stop sinning by breaking off the affair."

The priest's words felt like a knife had been plunged through Sofia's heart. She did not say anything.

"Our sins are not truly forgiven until we take up our penance," the priest said. Then his voice softened. "Turn to God, not man, in your hour of pain and suffering. You may now leave."

"Thank you, Father," Sofia said, then left.

CHAPTER NINE

Kat was pulled out of her sleep by the sound of loud knocking on the door. It took her a moment to remember where she was.

"Kat, Kat," she heard a woman's voice say urgently at the door.

The room was almost dark, as dawn had not yet fully broken.

Kat sat up in bed and blinked. As her eyes adjusted, she saw Blaine next to her. He was rubbing his eyes and looking as confused and disoriented as she was. Then suddenly she realized she wasn't in her own home in Lindsay, Kansas, but instead she was in Deborah's house in Italy.

She jumped out of bed and said, "Come in, come in."

Deborah opened the door. "I'm really sorry to wake you up." She was in her pajamas, her hair sticking up in all directions. But it was the look on her face that alarmed Kat. Her eyes were wide and her features were creased in fear.

"I just got a call from Luigi. You know his friend, the man he was talking about last night, the one who was meant to be his best man, Bruno Lombardi? He was murdered last night."

"Oh my goodness," Kat said.

Blaine had been half-asleep, but he quickly sat upright when he heard what Deborah said, and was instantly wide awake.

"I hate to ask this..." Deborah said as she bit at one of her nails and looked awkward. "But since you helped solve the murder of the coed who was having an affair with my ex-husband, and the other murders in Lindsay... I was wondering if you and Blaine would come along with us to Sardinia?"

Kat walked over to Deborah and hugged her. "Of course. I'll be there alongside you every step of the way, but I'm not sure how much help I'll be. I'm in a foreign country. I barely speak the language. Do you not have faith in the police here?"

"We do," Deborah said. "Although some of them can be bribed if the price is right. It may have something to do with organized crime, since Bruno was so rich. Who knows? But in any case, I'll just feel better with you there. You have a sharp mind. You know what to look for. I think you could really be of some help, Kat, and I know it would make Luigi feel better."

"How is he holding up?" Blaine asked.

Deborah let out a little sob and a single tear trickled down her cheek, which she quickly wiped away. "Not well. I have to be strong for him. Bruno was his oldest and best friend. As much as he had his arrogant ways, the two of them teased each other a lot. I think Luigi was the only person Bruno could really be humble with. It was a special friendship. A special, special friendship."

"That's so sad," Kat said. "I'm truly sorry for Luigi."

"Yes," Deborah said. "I'm really sorry about this, too. This isn't how you wanted to spend your trip."

"Oh, don't be silly!" Kat quickly said. "Our trip is nothing. A man's life has ended. That's certainly more important than our trip."

"Yes, but..." Deborah began to say.

"Say no more, Deborah," Blaine interrupted. "We're here to help and support you, and we're happy to do it. In the good times and the bad times."

Deborah burst into tears. "You're such good friends."

Kat gave her another hug, feeling her own heart hurting on her friend's behalf. What a sad thing to have happened, and just before their wedding. It was supposed to be a joyous occasion.

Deborah wiped her eyes as she pulled away. "I'm going to get dressed and put my warpaint on. I need to be strong for Luigi. He's called a driver to come and pick us up and take us to a private airport where we will meet him. Then we'll head to Sardinia on his plane. I'm sorry about the short notice."

"Not a problem," Blaine said, "We'll be ready to go when you are."

"Luigi's anxious to get over there as soon as possible. It was Bruno's wife who called, Chiari. She found him when he was late getting back from his tasting of a new wine release. He died in his wine cellar."

"How horrible," said Kat with a shiver. "Poor woman."

"Yes, it's so sad." Deborah said. "I hope we can all offer her some support. Luigi says she can be quite shy at times and doesn't have that many friends. I doubt if she has a good support network."

Kat began to arrange her outfit for the flight. "Thankfully, Blaine and I were too tired after the dinner last night to unpack many of our things. It will only take us a few minutes to get ready."

"I have to pack myself," Deborah said. "I'd better get a move on. We only have twenty minutes or so before the driver arrives. Feel free to grab some bread from the kitchen. There's cheese in the fridge, if you'd like. Or cold cuts. Or cereal. I doubt we'll be able to eat for a while."

With that said, they all rushed around to get ready, packing, and throwing together quick breakfasts for themselves.

Soon they stood in the hallway surrounded by their suitcases. "I don't know if I've got too little or too much," Deborah said. "I don't know how long we'll be there. Oh, that reminds me. I need to ask the neighbors if they can feed Primo for a couple days." Deborah rushed out of the room and headed next door.

Blaine and Kat looked at each other, and Blaine ran his hand up and down Kat's back. It was the first time they'd been able to slow down and breathe since waking up that morning.

"Well…" Kat said. "What can I say?" She didn't know what to say at all, but the situation seemed so strange she felt compelled to say something. "This is unexpected."

"Indeed," Blaine said. "The curveballs life throws…"

Kat sighed. "I just feel for Deborah. She went through so much in Lindsay. Now she comes here to start a new life. Everything starts out good, and soon it's like a fairytale, marrying a wonderful man who lives in a castle, for goodness' sake! That's what I wanted for her. Not this." Kat felt a little tearful and hung her head with a feeling of great sadness.

Blaine gave her a hug. "People would kill for friends like you. Oh, gosh, sorry, bad choice of words. What I meant to say was you're such a wonderful friend…" He buried his face in her hair for a moment. "I guess… we can't predict or control what life has in store for us. But being good friends, that's a choice. And it makes everything easier."

Kat looked up at him and managed a small smile, in spite of the heavy feeling in her heart. "Yes, you're right. Love and friendship make the road feel a little smoother." She thought of Bruno's poor wife. She couldn't imagine what it would be like to find Blaine dead. She wasn't sure she'd ever recover. "I don't know how I can be of any help in the investigation, like Deborah hopes. But I do know I can support Deborah, so hopefully I can be of use to this lady Chiari, too. She probably needs all the friends and support she can get right now."

Blaine nodded. "And though I don't know Luigi well, I'll be there for him, too."

Kat smiled up at him, then wrapped him up in a great big hug. "I'm so glad I married you."

They heard a car pull up outside as Deborah rushed back in the house. "The driver's here," she said quickly. "Come on, let's get these suitcases out to him." She lugged hers out the door and hurried to the waiting limousine.

"The next door neighbors say they're too scared of Primo to feed him, and anyway, they're going on vacation tomorrow." She bit her lip and looked down the street. "I don't know anyone else, and I wouldn't feel comfortable asking them. I think I'll just have to bring him along."

Kat nodded. "Sounds like a plan. That's one benefit of having a private plane, I suppose. It's not too complicated to bring him."

The driver got out and helped Blaine load the suitcases in the trunk.

"Yep," said Deborah. "I'll just go back in and get some dog biscuits."

"Okay," Kat replied. "Is there anything you want me to do?"

Deborah looked stressed. "Um… no, I think we're good to go."

Within a few minutes, they were all loaded in the limousine, Primo included, and rushing to the airport. The driver had obviously been told to step heavily on the gas. People seemed to be quite lax about seatbelts in Italy. Kat hadn't seen Deborah or Luigi use theirs. But now, even Deborah was raising her eyebrows and buckling up. "We don't want two tragedies in one day," she said, shaking her head.

The Italian scenery, bathed in the lilac light of dawn, wasn't so easy to appreciate when they were bumping along unpaved backroads. They were obviously taking some kind of shortcut, and it led through an impoverished looking agricultural area, where everyone seemed to have pickup trucks parked outside their small concrete homes.

Soon they reached the private airport. It was larger than Kat expected. Someone in uniform rushed toward the limousine as the driver brought it to a stop, and then rushed just as fast in the other direction with their bags.

They were led through a large shiny hangar with ten or fifteen small planes inside, and then out onto the tarmac.

"There it is," Deborah said, pointing to a plane with the steps lowered down onto the tarmac. The words 'Gulfstream G550' were printed on the side of the plane which had seven windows on each side of the fuselage.

When Kat had heard the words 'private plane' she'd been a little worried that it would be some tiny thing that would feel small and unsafe in the air. When she saw the big Gulfstream, however, she let out a private sigh of relief. With its huge wingspan and sturdy body, it certainly wasn't small. They watched the man with their bags store them in the hold of the plane.

Deborah, Blaine, and Kat hurriedly walked up the steps, Primo trotting along obediently behind them.

"Oh, thank heavens you're here," Luigi said, meeting them inside the plane. He gave Deborah a quick hug and a kiss, but there was no time for any more pleasantries. "I'm going to be in the cockpit with the pilot. Please make yourselves comfortable here in the main cabin. If you'd like, Martina will get you some coffee." Before they had a chance to reply, he rushed towards the cockpit saying, "Come on, let's get out of here."

The interior of the plane was sleek, luxurious, and modern. A deep plush gray carpet made it soft underfoot, while a creamy white and gray color scheme gave a soft effect to the reclining chairs and coffee tables.

"Hi, I'm Martina," a stewardess said. She was in her thirties and wore an attractive cream and gray uniform to match the décor of the plane.

"Hi, Martina, nice to see you again," Deborah said. "I wish it could be under better circumstances."

"Yes, my condolences to you," she said kindly. "Now, Mr. Luigi is very anxious to leave immediately, so if you could all please take a recliner seat and buckle up, then we can takeoff. The coffee is almost ready. I'll get it for you once we're airborne."

CHAPTER TEN

The flight was short, taking just under one hour. Primo had curled up in a corner and slept through the whole flight. Most of the time, Kat, Blaine, and Deborah talked about Bruno and Chiari while sipping their coffee.

"I've only met him once," Deborah said. "But he and Luigi talked on the phone every single week. Usually Sunday afternoons. You know, like how you make calls to family? I truly believe they saw themselves as family, even though they weren't related. They could talk for hours and hours, about wine, politics, books, new gadgets, and all sorts of things. They were truly like brothers."

"What a great thing, to have such a good friend," Blaine said.

"Yes," Deborah said, getting a little teary-eyed. "I was so excited to see him again. Luigi couldn't wait to spend the few days with him leading up to our wedding. They're both so busy, what with their vineyards, and all the publicity Bruno does. They were never able to get together as often as they'd have liked." She swallowed and looked toward the cockpit. "If I know Luigi, I expect he'll be regretting that now. All those 'reasons' they both had for not making the trip... well, they'll seem really insignificant now."

That struck a chord with Kat. It had taken a wedding to get her to come to Italy and see Deborah, who had become one of her best friends. Although, of course, she had a busy life back in Lindsay, and she and Blaine couldn't go jetting off every weekend, but she took what Deborah was saying to heart. "We let life get in the way sometimes, don't we?"

"And the sad thing about it is that so much of it doesn't really mean anything," Deborah said. "We fill our time with so much stuff. We're always busy, so, so busy. But I'll bet half of it isn't really that important."

"That's so true," Blaine said.

"We're all lucky that we have jobs we love," Kat said. "That certainly helps us know we're not whiling our lives away."

"Yes," Deborah said. "But… that's not really what I was getting at. See, I don't think it matters if you don't enjoy your job. Someone has to pump gas. Someone has to check the groceries, and most people don't find those jobs particularly fulfilling. But what matters is priorities. Remembering what's important, each and every day, instead of getting swept up in the… I don't really know what to call it. The noise, I guess? The noise of life."

"I see what you mean," said Kat. "Remembering what's truly important, every single day."

Deborah smiled ruefully. "Yes. Easier said than done, isn't it?"

"Certainly is," Blaine agreed. "It's very easy to get caught up in the stuff."

The flight felt even shorter than it was, and Kat was surprised as they began to descend. "Wow, that was quick."

They landed on a small airstrip right by the coast, tucked into the Sardinian countryside among rows and rows of vineyards.

"This is Bruno's private airstrip" Deborah said. "Luigi told me it's just a short drive to the house."

"Oh, is that it?" Kat said, pointing to a huge, classic looking Italian mansion.

Deborah nodded. "I think so."

There were three luxurious cars waiting for them at the airstrip. The drivers were standing at a distance, smoking cigarettes and chatting, but they stubbed them out as soon as the airplane door opened. They rushed forward to get the suitcases, while Primo bounded down the folding stairs, followed by everyone else.

Luigi went over to the cars and spoke to one of the drivers in Italian. Kat wished she spoke it. It was such a rhythmic and beautiful language.

Before long, they were ready to go. Kat and Blaine were in one car, which had luxurious cream leather seating. Deborah, Luigi and Primo were in the second. Luigi's face was grave as he stood beside the car and looked around at the surrounding vineyards. Kat could only imagine how his heart was breaking in that very painful moment, looking at the special place his friend loved most in all the world, but his friend was gone. After all their luggage had been loaded into the third car they began their drive up through the vineyards toward the mansion.

As they got closer, Kat noticed part of the mansion looked centuries old, while one wing, which looked out at the sea, was sleek and modern. It was quite a strange mix, but certainly made the place look grand and imposing. On both sections, the gold intricate railings across the veranda were the same, somehow uniting the entirely different parts of the building.

Kat turned her head to see what the view would be like from the veranda, and saw that it was absolutely stunning. The vineyards rolled all the way across the landscape to the coast, giving way to a fantastic view of the Mediterranean, a deep blue that was glittering in the morning sunlight.

Soon they arrived at the grand entrance, which was located in the older classical part of the mansion. They were led into a large kitchen and dining room, which was filled with people, cooking, eating, and drinking. Kat was quite taken aback.

"Luigi!" A beautiful dark-haired woman rushed towards him and embraced him, sobbing. "Luigi..." Then she said something in Italian that Kat didn't understand.

Kat watched, feeling heartbroken. She assumed the woman must be Chiari, Bruno's wife. Kat looked at Deborah, who wiped away a little tear. Primo nuzzled into Deborah's side, and she reached down to gently pet him.

"Chiari, I am so sorry," Luigi said. "This is my wife-to-be, Deborah, and our friends, Kat and Blaine."

"Hello," Chiari said in a heavy Italian accent, though she didn't quite look them in the eye. She motioned towards the people in the kitchen and said, "Here is my family. They have just come from Lazio." She turned to Luigi and said something in Italian.

Luigi turned to them. "Chiari and I need to speak privately for a few minutes. She said you can all sit down at the table and eat."

Deborah smiled. "Absolutely. You two take as long as you need."

Chiari gave them a distracted smile, then walked out of the kitchen with Luigi following her. She led him through a hallway, through the salon, and into a back room. Then she opened a heavy door, with steps that led downwards. "Here," she said. They spoke in Italian from then on.

"His wine cellar," Luigi said, tears in his eyes.

"Yes," Chiari said. She'd cried for so long she felt numb. She wondered if she'd ever be able to cry again. "This is where... where I found him."

She turned on the light, and they walked down the stairs together.

Luigi felt claustrophobic, and, all of a sudden, so angry that he could break every bottle in the cellar if they hadn't been so precious to Bruno. "No," he said, then louder, "No!"

"Right here," Chiari said, walking to where the table and chairs had been. "He apparently was sitting here, drinking his new wine release. He was so excited about it. He had fallen off his chair when I found him lying on the floor. The police took it all, the table, the chair, and the bottle, for evidence."

"That was a quick response," Luigi said.

"Yes. Well, given who Bruno was…"

Luigi shook his head and paced the floor. "How… how was he killed?"

"At first they thought it was a heart attack. But the doctor said the way he looked was more symptomatic of poisoning. That's when the police were called."

"Poisoning?" said Luigi, startled. "But…" His mind raced. "Do you know what kind of poison?"

"Not yet," Chiari said. "The doctor and the coroner will find out and tell us, but no, I know nothing yet."

Luigi shook his head, looking around at the bottles of wine. Bruno had been murdered, right in the heart of the place he loved the most. A place where he should have been safe. "Who could have done it? Not many people have access to this room."

"This is the thing," said Chiari. "The vineyard manager and a couple of the workers have access. Then there's just me and Bruno. He doesn't even allow the house cleaners and staff to come down here. He insists that the vineyard manager clean it after it has been used."

"Is the vineyard manager still Gabriele Ferrari?" Luigi asked. He had been the manager for ten years now, and Luigi had met him on a few occasions. Bruno always sung his praises.

"Yes," Chiari said. "I am sure it is not him. He would never want to harm Bruno." Her voice cracked. "Anyway, I cannot even begin to think of all this. It makes me too fearful. Whoever did it may very well want to kill me, too. I will leave the task of solving this terrible crime up to the police, and hide in the bosom and protection of my family."

She knew that many of the family members were only there because they knew she would inherit all of Bruno's money, and wanted to be sweet to her so she would drop a portion of it into their hands. But none of them knew about little Diego Ossani-Lombardi. She was hoping he would not show up on the doorstep with his devil of a mother.

"My fiancée Deborah has brought her matron of honor along, Kat Denham. She is an author by trade, but has been instrumental in solving a few murders in Lindsay, Kansas, which is where they come from in the United States. Deborah and I think she might be able to help."

Chiari nodded. "Anything for Bruno. We must get justice for him."

Luigi nodded. "We will. Between the police and Kat, we have a good thing going. And if Kat cannot solve it, we will hire more investigators. Justice will be served for Bruno, Chiari. You can trust me on that."

Chiari gave him a hug. "You were his best friend, Luigi. He loved you. Do you know that?"

"Yes," Luigi said, a lump rising in his throat. "I do. I wish we could have had our wedding just a few days earlier, so he could have been there."

Chiari nodded. "He will be there in spirit. He was so happy for you, that you found yourself a lovely woman to grow old with."

Luigi wiped his eyes. "Yes. We celebrated our victories together. But Chiari, you have lost your life partner. How will you go on? What help do you need?"

Chiari straightened her back and held her head high. "I will go on, for Bruno's memory. He would not want to see me go down. I have my family to help me." Truthfully, she doubted they would be any help at all, but it would be disloyal to say so. "I will be fine. With God's and Mother Mary's help, I will be fine."

"Okay," Luigi said, not entirely convinced. "As long as you're sure, Chiari. Make sure you call me if you need anything, anything at all. You could even come to stay with us, if you want. Whatever you need."

"You are a generous man."

"No," said Luigi. "I see you as family. It is nothing. Nothing is too much for you to ask for. Do you understand?"

"Yes," Chiari said. "Thank you, Luigi. It means a lot to me. But you must make sure your fiancée is happy first."

Luigi broke into a laugh. "Oh, Chiari, you do expect the worst from people. She has already cried on your behalf. She wants to befriend you and make sure you are happy and cared for."

Chiari had found it very difficult to trust any woman, since Sofia had betrayed her so spectacularly. So this declaration from Luigi did not mean much to her. "She is being most kind," she said evenly.

"She is a very good-hearted person," Luigi said. "As are Kat and her husband Blaine. Shall we go and see them now? I expect Kat will want to start investigating as soon as possible."

"Yes," Chiari said. "Any help is good help."

CHAPTER ELEVEN

Soon they were in the salon, sitting with a huge spread of food in front of them. Chiari's family had brought copious amounts of food and drink with them. Consequently, the large marble coffee table was covered with bottles of alcohol and all kinds of cakes and snacks.

"I will not drink wine," Chiari said, and poured herself a glass of a creamy-looking liquid.

"What's that?" Luigi asked, looking at the bottle. "Guappa?" Chiari handed him the bottle. "Buffalo milk with brandy, aged for three years," he said, reading the label.

"I can drink the whole bottle," said Chiari. "Please, it makes you eat and drink. This can make life be... less terrible."

Kat was thinking hard about the murder already. She saw how much pain it was causing Luigi, who was trying to put on a brave face for Chiari, and by extension Deborah, who was trying to put on a brave face for Luigi. Luigi had already mentioned that the murder had happened in the wine cellar, and that only the vineyard manager and a couple of workers had access.

Chiari became quite insistent that they all pour themselves drinks.

"I'll try the Guappa," Deborah said. Primo was curled up at her feet and she ruffled his neck. Blaine and Kat followed suit. Then followed a somewhat uncomfortable silence as they all stared into space or into their drinks.

"May I ask you a question, Chiari?" Kat asked. She felt quite nervous, but her urge to solve the mystery of Bruno's death spurred her on.

"Of course," Chiari said.

"Luigi told me that the vineyard manager had access to the cellar, as well as a couple of workers. Do you think any of them could have been involved in the murder?"

"I do not understand," Chiari said.

Deborah jumped in to translate, and spoke fluently in Italian. Then Chiari spoke back to her and Deborah translated back to English for Kat. "She says the vineyard manager is a good man and would have no reason to hurt Bruno. She does not know who else has access to the wine cellar, but thinks perhaps someone was paid to enter by one of Bruno's enemies. She cannot think of any other explanation."

The conversation continued with Deborah as the translator. "You say one of Bruno's enemies," Kat said. "Do you have any idea who those enemies might be?"

"Perhaps Vito Rizzo," Deborah translated. "He is a competing winemaker here in Sardinia, and was always jealous of Bruno. Bruno won all the awards for wine and was beloved by the press and critics. Vito Rizzo always came in second in tasting competitions and was known for complaining about it. He is also known for his violent temper.

"Apparently once he strangled his own vineyard manager for making a mistake. The vineyard manager did not die, but was very shaken. Rizzo paid him off to keep from taking his story to the press, but news travels fast within the wine community of Sardinia.

Everyone knows what he did."

"Okay," Kat said as she processed the information. "So perhaps he put a worker in your vineyards to deliver the poison. Is that what you're thinking?"

Once translated by Deborah, Chiari nodded. Then she looked distinctly uncomfortable.

"What is wrong?" Kat asked.

Chiari burst into tears and spoke thickly and very fast. Luigi patted Chiari on the knee, looking awkward and sorrowful. Deborah translated, and Kat was very impressed with how fluent she'd become in Italian, given the rather short period of time she'd been in Italy.

"She says there is something else she has to say, but it is very shameful. She wants us to close all the doors, so there is no possibility of her family hearing."

Luigi and Blaine both jumped up and closed the numerous doors to the salon.

"She also wants us to all swear we will not repeat this," Deborah said. "She does not want anyone to know, especially the press. She does not want to ruin Bruno's reputation or her own. Also, she has only recently found this information out, and it is a very raw wound for her."

"Okay," said Kat. "Please tell her none of us will repeat it."

Deborah did so, but then said, "She wants us all to assure her of that."

Luigi and Blaine promised not to tell anyone, and then Deborah did too, speaking in Italian.

Chiari poured herself another Guappa and looked nervous. "I had a housekeeper named Sofia. She was my best friend for the two years she was here. Then she left because she was pregnant. I have recently found out that she was pregnant with Bruno's child, and the child is now thirteen years old."

Luigi gasped, dropping his head into his hands. Then Chiari and he spoke in Italian which Deborah continued to translate.

"She asked him if he did not know, since she thought Bruno told him everything. He replied he did not. He thought they shared everything too. He is very shocked and saddened. He thought Bruno was so devoted to Chiari he would never do such a thing. Chiari says she had thought so, too, but they were both wrong."

Then Chiari continued. "She says that the child even has Bruno's surname, as well as Sofia's," Deborah translated. "And that the child wrote her a letter, saying that she was preventing Bruno from coming to live with Sofia and Diego, his real family."

Tears streamed down Chiari's face as she took the letter from her dress pocket and handed it to Luigi. He read it, looking very disturbed, shaking his head over and over again.

Chiari continued and Deborah translated, "She says it sounds like Bruno was telling them lies about her, and that he wanted to leave, but she was preventing him. Perhaps Sofia got tired about hearing this, and finally snapped?"

"Oh," Kat said. "I'm so sorry."

Chiari sniffed. Deborah translated, "I will be okay. It is only... I do not know what kind of man I was married to. Perhaps he made one mistake and Sofia is lying to the child. Perhaps Sofia is lying altogether because she wants to get her hands on Bruno's money and estate, and the child is not really Bruno's." Then she burst into tears again. "I don't understand what is happening with my life."

Deborah stood up and then sat next to Chiari. She gave her a hug and spoke to her in a soothing voice. She gestured toward Kat. Kat guessed she was saying that everything would be okay and that Kat was going to do her utmost to catch the killer.

Kat was beginning to feel the pressure. Who could have predicted that a fun vacation with a glorious happily-ever-after wedding, would have turned into this? But for Chiari's benefit, she forced herself to find an optimistic smile. She couldn't imagine the turmoil and mixed emotions poor Chiari must be feeling.

To not know whether her husband had been lying to her all these years... To wonder if their whole relationship had been a lie... And then to find the man dead and not be able to get any answers. To wonder if her own life was now in danger. It was a lot for one person to handle.

"We will work this out the best we can," Kat said. "Though we can't bring your husband back, at least we can find out who did this and bring them to justice. We won't stop until we do."

Deborah translated, and Chiari gave her a wobbly smile.

Kat wondered how long this was all going to take. If necessary, she and Blake could extend their stay. They'd have to change their flights, but their visas allowed them to stay for up to three months in Italy, so that wasn't a problem. She was sure Lacie and Tyler would stick around to look after the dogs. Blaine should be able to get some extra vacation time, since he'd barely taken any since he'd won his election, and the Deputy DAs could step in and cover for him.

If there was a problem with him staying, Kat would just have to stay on alone. She needed to continue writing, as some of her books were on pre-release and needed to be completed by a certain date, but she could continue that in her own time. It would be a good way to distract herself from the grim murder investigation, and escape for a little while.

Luigi and Chiari spoke briefly in Italian. Deborah translated. "Luigi said he knows Bruno and his brother were not that close, but wondered if the brother, Salvatore, would be coming. Chiari says he will be coming soon, but he had to find someone to take care of his

Bed and Breakfast in Esporico, and he's finding it quite hard to find someone to fill his shoes."

Luigi looked quite disapproving. Kat thought that perhaps Bruno had told Luigi all kinds of bad things about his brother. Perhaps Salvatore was an unsavory character? Then her mind jumped to the fact that perhaps he might inherit, given Bruno's death, rather than Chiari.

"Are Bruno's parents still alive?" Kat asked.

"No," Luigi replied in English. "Their mother died when they were very young. Their father passed many years ago."

"Were the vineyards and this home his?"

"Yes," said Luigi. "This is a family place."

Kat ventured her idea, though rather tentatively. "Chiari, do you know who the estate passes to now?"

Deborah translated Chiari's response. "Me, of course, as his wife. I have not seen his will, but surely it must be me." But she had begun nibbling on the skin at the side of one of her long fake nails, and looking worried.

"I was just wondering, given that it is a family estate, if Salvatore might stand to inherit, and that he might have access to the cellar."

Chiari looked outraged and raised her voice when she spoke.

"She said Salvatore would never do such a thing. And he will not inherit anyway," Deborah translated.

A horrible thought struck Kat. Since Chiari was so incensed, she was tempted not to say it. But the murder investigation had to continue, regardless of anyone's hurt feelings. She didn't like being shouted at, but was prepared to be. "What if you died? Who would the estate pass to then? Salvatore?"

Deborah winced before she translated it, but she duly did so. Chiari, sure enough, shouted, and then cried.

Deborah translated, "She says do you suggest Salvatore killed his own brother, and then would come to kill me, his first love? Do you want to take away everyone in the world from me? First Sofia takes my husband away, then a murderer does. I have no one. Salvatore is a good man. A very, very kind and gentle man. Kat, I think we should stop now. I think she needs to rest."

"You're right," Kat said. She was very intrigued about Chiari being Salvatore's first love, but realized it would have to be pursued another day. Chiari was sobbing and pouring herself another Guappa.

Kat started to feel guilty. "Can you tell her I'm really sorry? I didn't mean to make her so upset. I just want to make sure we don't miss anyone when we're looking into the murder. I really am sorry, though. Maybe we can talk more tomorrow?"

Deborah translated and Chiari's sobs quietened to sniffs. Then she spoke in a quiet voice.

"She says she understands, and appreciates what you are doing," Deborah translated. "Just please, try to be gentle with her. She is not coping very well and feels very fragile. She is under even more pressure from entertaining her family."

Kat felt very sad for Chiari. Even after her husband had been murdered, she still felt an obligation to entertain her family and friends. That told her all she needed to know about Chiari's family dynamics. She wanted to reach out and hug Chiari, but she was sure that would be quite inappropriate, especially given how she had just upset her.

"I'm so sorry," she said again. "Rest assured I intend do my absolute best for Bruno."

Chiari gave her a grateful, though tear-stained, smile.

CHAPTER TWELVE

Kat was very glad they weren't putting more pressure on Chiari by staying over and requiring more 'entertaining,' like her family did. Instead, the four of them, with Luigi's help, made arrangements to stay at the Hotel Pitrizza. Luigi had an old friend who owned it, and Luigi and Bruno had often gone there for dinner and drinks after a round of golf.

While they were still sipping their Guappas, Luigi had ordered a rental car. "I can't stand taxis," he said. "You always have to be prepared to wait until they are ready to come and get you."

Soon they were driving out of the vast Lombardi estate and toward Costa Smaralda, where the hotel was located. It was a short drive, but very scenic, with excellent views of the glittering Mediterranean.

The hotel itself was right on the coast, a handful of luxury stone buildings constructed against the natural rock formations at the seafront.

"Wow, this is really something," Deborah said, but in a muted sort of way. None of them could muster up any joy given the circumstances. She looked at Primo worriedly. "Are you sure they're okay with dogs?"

"Not usually," Luigi said, "but they said they'll make an exception."

Luigi drove up to the entrance and a valet opened his door and indicated he would take the car. As Luigi walked towards the hotel entrance, he stopped and gripped onto one of the grand columns supporting the portico. He stared at the fountain, its relaxing trickling sound echoing around the marble atrium.

Then he stared vacantly at the view of the Mediterranean Sea beyond. He looked all around, seemingly taking in everything, as if it was the first time he'd ever been there, and he was very entranced by all of it. Kat, Deborah, and Blaine walked towards the reception desk with Luigi following, while the bell staff wheeled their suitcases into the hotel lobby.

"Welcome back to the Pitrizza, Mr. Giordano," one of the staff members said to Luigi.

Luigi snapped out of his reverie. "Oh, yes, yes, thank you." He walked up to the others. "I do apologize," he said. "This is the first time I have been here without Bruno. It has caused me to suffer a great sadness."

"We could get another hotel, if you like?" Deborah suggested. "One without so many memories."

"No," Luigi said, then his face brightened up. "No thank you, darling. You are most kind to think of me, but I will be fine. I want to be here. I want to remember Bruno. We will have a special dinner tonight, to give him a good send off. We will drink. We will eat. We will be merry. That is what Bruno liked to do. Then seeking justice must resume in the morning."

Kat nodded. "That sounds like a good plan."

They checked in, and were led to their rooms by a staff member who knew Luigi personally. They chatted in Italian, and Kat could just make out that they were talking about wine. The word 'vino' was easy enough to remember. The staff member also made a big fuss over Primo, and Kat saw that Deborah was visibly relaxing.

The hotel suites were more like villas, spread across the gorgeous coastal landscape. They were all connected by a luxurious and large outdoor area, with an infinity pool that appeared to splash over the edge and right into the sea. It had been edged with an abundance of blue tiles – azure and sky blue and cobalt and indigo and royal blue and navy – until the entire pool looked like the sea itself. From the pool area, a grand staircase flanked with palm, fuchsia, and bougainvillea plants, led down towards a white sand beach. But they took the other direction, toward the villas. It was a beautiful pathway, with pale gravel that crunched pleasingly underfoot.

"I hope you will love our facilities," the hotel staffer said to Kat, Blaine, and Deborah. "Will you be joining us for dinner tonight?"

"Yes," Blaine said with a smile. "I believe we are planning a feast in honor of a dear friend of Luigi's."

"Ah, yes, a feast! Well, that can certainly be arranged."

"It is going to be in honor of Bruno Lombardi," Luigi said quietly. "He has passed away."

The hotel staffer stopped walking. "No. Mr. Giordano, you cannot be telling the truth."

Luigi spoke in Italian, his voice full of feeling.

The hotel staffer replied with the same level of feeling, and actually wiped a tear away. He said something in Italian, and then turned to the others. "Mr. Lombardi was a truly wonderful man. We hosted him here many times. Many, many times. In his honor, we will prepare the largest feast Hotel Pitrizza has ever seen. You do not need to concern yourself with the arrangements."

Then, still looking slightly disturbed, he led them to their villas, which were adjoined by a courtyard and a pool that rippled and shone in the sunlight. Both villas were made of stone, in a mix of tans and warm beiges. The old-time feel of this was contrasted with white sleek décor everywhere else. The doors were modern and patent white, and the lounges were sleek and white, too.

The white theme continued inside, and everything looked fresh and clean. Kat and Blaine had a huge living room, a shining white-tiled bathroom, and a bedroom with a white four poster bed and a two-person jacuzzi, set up in a perfect position so they could watch the widescreen television from the bath.

"Oh my goodness," Kat said to Blaine, once Deborah and Luigi had gone to their own suite to unpack. "This is quite something."

"Isn't it just," Blaine said, looking out the bedroom window that gave them an incredible view of the Mediterranean. "Bruno and Luigi sure knew how to live it up. I'm loathe to even look up the room rate for this place. I told Luigi that I'd pay, but he wouldn't hear of it. He said it was on him because of how we've been inconvenienced."

"He's a good man, isn't he? I'm really happy for Deborah."

"That he is," Blaine said. "More of a gentleman you'd be hard pressed to meet." He sat down on the bed beside her.

Kat snuggled into him. "Except you, of course."

"You're too kind."

"I sure hope someone will find Bruno's murderer soon, whether that's us, or the police, or whomever. As much as I'd like to, we can't stay here indefinitely. Of course, I can work from here and write my books on my laptop, but you'll have to get back to your DA duties soon, won't you?"

"Yes," he said. "But if we need to stay here a few more days, I can get the deputies to appear in court for me. I'm certainly not leaving you here on your own."

"I can…"

"Kat, you're a strong woman," he said as he interrupted her. "The strongest I've ever known, but there is no way I could let you stay here, on your own, searching for a murderer. Your life could be in danger."

"But I'm…"

"I know I can't stop you from investigating. Half of me wishes I could, just to protect you. I don't want anything to happen to you, and investigating murders is inherently dangerous. But the other half? I'm proud of you. So proud I could burst. So I can't stop you, and I won't try, but you do have to let me be there for you. If something happened to you, and I wasn't here to protect you, I'd never be able to forgive myself."

Kat smiled. "I'm sure I'll be all right, but I really appreciate it. And I have to admit, being here is much more nerve-racking than back in Lindsay. At least there I was on my home turf. I knew where I was. Here, I'm disoriented. And it's likely the killer knows every nook and cranny of the place. They must if they managed to sneak poison into Bruno's wine, in his own cellar. Or at least that's the coroner's preliminary report, from what Luigi found out. That's a pretty amazing feat. Unless…"

"Unless what?"

Kat thought for a moment. "Nothing. Crazy idea. Now, do you know what Luigi and Deborah have planned for the rest of the day?"

They met out by the pool a short while later.

"I hope the room is to your satisfaction," Luigi said. "Lovely place, isn't it?"

"Yes it is," Kat said

"It certainly is," Blaine said. "How much do I…"

"Nothing!" Luigi said firmly, giving Blaine a brotherly pat on the back. "Now, do you play golf?"

Blaine smiled. "Infrequently. When I'm lucky enough to get the time."

"Brilliant!" said Luigi. "I'll make arrangements for us to play at the Pevero Golf Club tomorrow, while these ladies investigate. I want to talk to Chiari about funeral arrangements, but otherwise, there's no point in me sitting here doing nothing. Bruno would not have approved."

Kat nodded. "It's good to keep yourself busy."

"Kat, why don't we walk down by the beach with Primo?" Deborah suggested, then laughed. "We can leave these two to talk about drives or clubs or tees or whatever these golf mad men love to chat about."

Kat laughed along. "I certainly don't want to be caught up in that conversation. The beach sounds like a great idea. Give me just a minute. I want to change into some sandals."

She did so, and put on some sunscreen as well. Deborah went inside her villa to get Primo, then she and Kat meandered up to the main infinity pool, and past it towards the beach.

"You know, I had an idea," said Kat. "It's a crazy one, and not pleasant to think about, but I don't think it can be overlooked."

"What is it?" Deborah asked.

"Well, of course we have to interview the vineyard manager. He's the one who prepared the bottle of wine for Bruno, so it would only make sense."

"Of course," said Deborah.

"And we need to also have a look into who else might have been able to get access to the wine cellar."

"Yes."

Kat paused, not sure she wanted to venture forth with her idea. It seemed disloyal. "But what about Chiari? She certainly would have had access."

"Yes, she would..." Deborah frowned. "I don't think it's likely she killed Bruno, though. Luigi said they always seemed to have a good relationship."

"Oh, come on," said Kat. "He's been having an affair for over thirteen years, and she's just received a note from his illegitimate son."

Deborah didn't look convinced. "It might have just been that this woman was trying to make a buck off of Bruno. It might not be true at all."

"Yes, but what if it is? Chiari could have decided to poison Bruno's wine because she found out about his affair."

"Not much of a crime of passion though, is it?" Deborah said. "You'd expect a shooting or a strangling or something like that. Not a method as calculated as poisoning."

Kat shrugged. "Perhaps she's more calculated. Wants to make sure she doesn't get caught."

Deborah shook her head. "I don't think so."

As they stepped onto the warm soft sand, Kat slipped her sandals off. She just loved the feeling of warm sand between her toes. "But why not?"

"I don't know," Deborah said. "I just have a hunch she didn't do it. She wasn't involved."

Deborah's insistence was starting to get a little on Kat's nerves. "You can't go on hunches. I mean, you can use them to go digging in a new direction or whatever, but you can't rule someone out from the investigation on a hunch. They're not reliable enough."

"Whatever you say," Deborah said, with a little laugh. "But mark my words, when you wrap this investigation up, it won't be Chiari being led away in handcuffs. I can feel that."

Kat smiled. "Time will tell, but I want to at least think about it. I can't rule her out just yet."

"Hmm. What about Salvatore?" said Deborah. "We'll have to find out if he stands to inherit or not. That would certainly provide a motive if it turns out he's the heir to Bruno's estate."

"Yes," Kat said. "Since he grew up on the Lombardi estate, he could have easily had someone that he knew, and was loyal to him, do his dirty work for him while he was miles away at his B AND B."

"Definitely. And what was that about Chiari being Salvatore's first love?"

"I heard that" said Kat. "I sure wasn't expecting that one. How did Chiari end up marrying his brother? That must have been painful for him."

Deborah nodded. "Perhaps painful enough to kill."

"But why now?" Kat mused. "It must be at least twenty years later."

Deborah shrugged. "You know the old saying, revenge is a dish best served cold."

"Well, he's definitely someone else we have to speak to. Chiari said he's having a problem finding someone to look after his B AND B." She looked at Deborah with bright eyes. "Perhaps we should go down there? Where did she say it was again?"

"Esporico," Deborah said. "Wherever that is."

Kat whipped out her cell phone and tapped in the word "Esprico." "It's a one and a half hour drive down the coast. We'll have time to go down, stay for a while, then come back up before dinner at 8:00. How does that sound?"

Deborah smiled. "It's your call, boss. I'm just the translator."

CHAPTER THIRTEEN

Kat always tried not to be too disparaging about bad neighborhoods – after all, people had to live there, work there, grow up there, and conduct their daily lives there, so she thought it was in poor taste to think badly about such neighborhoods. But Esporico really tested her limits.

It was a rickety old seaside town, with old wooden buildings and concrete block houses with weeping black stains, caused by rain. The beach was a far cry from the pristine white sand at the hotel where they were staying. Deborah and Kat drove the rental car past a river leading to the sea, which was crammed full of empty plastic drink bottles, food wrappers, and other trash.

Similar items were strewn all along a trail leading down to the lapping shoreline where the sea frothed onto the dirty sand. Earlier they'd turned off the air-conditioner in their car and opened the windows to let the fresh smell of the sea breeze in, but as they drove into Esporico, the mixed stench of rubbish, seaweed, and dead fish filled their nostrils.

Deborah parked the car in a sad little parking lot by the beach front, and before they'd even stepped out of the car, they were swarmed by a group of little bare-chested boys between ten and twelve. They had on shorts and flip flops that were falling apart, and clutched various handcrafts and seashells.

"Hello, ladies," one said in a fake American accent. "Welcome to Italy. Let me give you a gift."

"No, take this one," another said. "It's much better!"

Deborah got out of the car and spoke to them in Italian in a gentle voice. They replied loudly and she replied sternly. She then let Primo out of the car and he immediately began to growl and bark, standing close to Deborah in a protective stance. Upon seeing Primo, the boys retreated, shouting at Kat and Deborah in Italian.

"What was that all about?" Kat asked.

"I told them maybe we'd buy later, then they insisted now, so I told them in no uncertain terms if they continued to bother us we certainly wouldn't be buying anything. They got scared by Primo, then said a few unsavory things as they left."

Kat watched them as they disappeared into a nearby street. "Shouldn't they be in school?"

"Yes." Deborah paused and looked around at the dirty beach, the rickety dock, and the people sitting listlessly outside their houses with nothing to do. She sighed deeply. "Poor kids."

"I wonder why Salvatore chose to live here," Kat wondered. "It's so very different from the Lombardi estate."

"I don't think this is the kind of place people choose to live," Deborah said.

"That's true enough," Kat said. "It's the kind of place where people get stuck. Its like they're at the bottom of the barrel and they have nowhere else to go."

"So, where did Salvatore's life go wrong?" Deborah wondered. "He started out his life living on a huge wine estate. His first love was Chiari, but then his brother married the love of his life, and he ended up here."

Kat shook her head. "We're missing something. Something's happened that we don't know about. The course of people's lives doesn't tend to vary dramatically like that, unless something unusual happens." She thought for a moment. "Perhaps he had a mental breakdown?"

"Maybe," said Deborah. "I guess we could ask Chiari."

"Yes," Kat agreed, "but first I'd like to see if we can find out from him. Even though I realize Chiari has to remain a suspect, I don't want to question her too much and upset her. Keeping that in mind, I'm going to behave as if she's innocent."

"Thank you," Deborah said. "I know that would mean a lot to Luigi."

"I guess we'd better try to find Salvatore. Maybe we could find a decent place to have coffee and a pastry, too."

"Let's try," said Deborah. "Come on, Primo."

Kat linked her arm with Deborah's as they walked toward where they thought the center of the village might be located. Primo went on ahead of them, but kept looking back to make sure they were okay.

"By the way, I didn't mean I was going to storm in there and accuse Chiari," Kat said with a laugh. "I was just trying to keep an open mind."

Deborah laughed with her. "Glad to hear that."

They soon arrived at a rickety little establishment called Gianna's Beach Bar. It looked incredibly depressing, and a woman, presumably Gianna, sat behind the counter with a very sour expression on her face as she looked down at her phone.

"Hi there," Kat said, putting on a smile and hoping it would be returned. "We're looking for a man named Salvatore Lombardi. Do you know where he might be?"

"Uh?" the woman said, barely glancing up from her phone.

"I think you'd better try," Kat said to Deborah.

Deborah stepped up to the bar and repeated what Kat had said, but in Italian. Gianna replied.

"Do you want a drink, Kat?" Deborah asked.

Kat looked at the slightly grubby place and didn't know what to say. It didn't look like any of the glasses had been properly washed. "Um, do they have Diet Coke?" She was hoping it would come from a bottle or can. "I'll just have a straw with it."

"*Due* Diet Coke," Deborah told Gianna.

Soon they were walking along a street, which was stained with some black and green slimy substance, and was adjacent to the dirty beach. Primo kept running down to the water, then scaring himself and running back again.

"Gianna said that Salvatore comes to drink there most days," Deborah said. "We can wait here for him to show up or we can head over to his B and B. She says the directions are quite complicated, because it's tucked away in some backstreets."

Kat nodded. "I think going to his B and B is a better idea. He might not come to the bar until late today, and we have to get back in time for Bruno's sending-off feast."

"You're right," Deborah said.

They turned to look at the little dingy streets and narrow alleyways. Kat took a deep breath. "Here goes nothing. Glad we've got Primo with us."

They made their way past mangy dogs who stared Primo down.

Primo growled back at them. There were old men sitting out in front of houses and a couple of old women scrubbing dirty clothes in large plastic basins. The alleyways between the houses were so narrow that several times they had to walk in single file. But there were spots of beauty here and there that they both admired. One of the tiny homes was painted in a dazzling azure, and had hanging baskets of flowers adorning practically the whole of its surface.

Someone else had a front door with a life-size painting of Mary painted on a gold background that made it look as if she was basking in the light of heaven. There was a lovely little chapel tucked away in a backstreet, where no one would expect it, and the singing voice of a child and an old woman came from inside. They were not perfectly in tune, but the effect was rather comforting.

Eventually they reached Salvatore's Bed and Breakfast. It was down one of the narrow lanes and was painted mint green. Or at least, once it been painted mint green, but most of the paint was now peeling. The words "Bed and Breakfast" were painted on the front in bold black letters.

"Oh, the sign is in English," Kat said, surprised.

"The Italians still call it Bed and Breakfast," Deborah explained, "although I'm not sure why. Anyway, shall we see if he's in?"

"Let's do it."

The interior was surprisingly nice and inviting. It was cramped, which was to be expected, given the street size, but it had a wonderful warm atmosphere. The walls were painted in a bright shade of saffron, while contrasting indigo and royal purple details were scattered through the room. A brown leather couch had indigo cushions, the heavy curtains were dark purple, and the lamp at the mahogany front desk had a bright purple shade. It wasn't modern. It wasn't luxurious. But it was cozy and beautiful, and had the most wonderful smell of herbs – perhaps thyme and rosemary, Kat thought. It looked exceptionally clean, too.

"Hi there," a young woman said from behind the desk. She looked to be about nineteen or twenty, and her dark hair was meticulously pulled back into a neat high ponytail which accentuated her huge, dark eyes. She stood up and smiled, and said in a near-perfect American accent, "Welcome to Salvatore's Bed and Breakfast. I'm Alessa. Have you come to stay with us?"

"Hi Alessa. No, we haven't," said Kat. "I have to say that's unfortunate, though! This place is beautiful."

Alessa blushed. "Well, I do my best. I like to try my hand at interior design."

"Your English is fantastic, too," said Deborah.

Alessa beamed from ear to ear. "You think so? I learned it in school, but mostly I taught myself by watching a lot of American movies."

Deborah smiled. "Word perfect, my dear. Is it okay for my dog to come inside?"

"Sure," Alessa said.

Deborah went to the door and beckoned to Primo who came trotting in.

Alessa's eyes widened when she saw the big dog. He did look ferocious. "What can I do for you?" she asked.

"Actually, we're here to see Salvatore," Kat said.

"Oh." Alessa bit her lip. "Well, that might be a problem, because he just left. He's going to visit a friend in the north of the island."

"Yes." Deborah smiled. "We know. We're friends with the person he's going to visit."

"Oh, right," Alessa said.

"Have you been working here a long time?" Kat asked.

"Two years."

Kat and Deborah exchanged a look.

"Do you think we could talk to you for a little while?" Kat asked. Someone's been murdered, and we…"

"I know," she said. "Bruno Lombardi's been murdered. Everyone knows."

"News travels fast in Sardinia, it seems!" Deborah said.

Alessa gave her a knowing smile. "I can find out what my neighbor's grandmother in the north ate for breakfast if I want." She winked. "Of course I can talk to you, although I am not sure I know any more than you do. Would you like to eat with me? I was about to make lunch."

"Oh, we wouldn't want to cause you too much trouble," said Kat.

"It's fine. You are very welcome!" Alessa grinned. "It's not that exciting though. Just an *Insalata Caprese*. How do you say that in English?"

Deborah and Kat laughed. "Insalata Caprese!" they both said together.

"It's actually one of my favorites," said Kat. "Mozzarella cheese slices with tomato slices, right?"

Alessa grinned. "Don't forget the basil, and I also like to add some olives. I was going to eat it with some focaccia we have left over from yesterday. Does that sound okay to you?"

"It sounds delicious," Deborah said.

Soon they were in the dining room, another quaint room that

reminded Kat of the dining room of a country Italian matriarch, and eating the delicious lunch Alessa had prepared. There was a door leading into a small courtyard, and Alessa set out a bowl of meat and leftovers from breakfast for Primo to eat out there.

"I'm sorry if this is a slightly awkward question, Alessa," Kat said, "but we're just trying to get to the bottom of this."

"Are you detectives?" Alessa asked, her eyes shining with excitement.

"Goodness, no," Kat said. "But we're investigators of a sort. A friend of Bruno's asked us to investigate."

"Oh, I see." Alessa nodded. "You don't think Salvatore did it, do you? He couldn't have done it, because he was here until just a half hour ago. He never leaves the town. He doesn't even have a car or a bike or any other vehicle. He had to get a taxi to go to the Lombardi estate this morning. I booked it for him myself. Besides, he's a nice man. He is very sad, but he is not a murderer."

"Very sad?" Deborah asked.

"He is very depressed," Alessa said. "He tells sad stories about the past all the time, and cannot look to the future. His favorite story to tell is how Chiari..." She trailed off, and her eyes went wide with alarm.

Kat nodded. "How Chiari was his first love?"

Alessa looked right and left, right and left, very rapidly, clearly panicking. "Um... Um..."

"It's okay, Alessa," Kat assured her. "It doesn't mean that we're going to think he's guilty. The truth will come out. We just need to get all the information we can about everyone. We know that Salvatore loved Chiari very much, but then she ended up marrying Bruno. Do you know how that happened?"

"Yes," Alessa said quietly. "Salvatore has told everybody, so it's not a secret." She explained about how Bruno and their father bullied Salvatore and turned Chiari against him.

"That was a long time ago," Deborah said. "But you say everybody knows this, and you've only been here two years. That must mean he's still talking about it."

"Yes. I would say he mentions Chiari's name at least once a day."

"From that I presume he's not had any other girlfriends," Kat said.

"Not that I know of," said Alessa. "I've told him to move on and find someone else, but he simply ignores me."

Kat paused. "Would you say he's still in love with her?"

Alessa nodded. "Absolutely."

CHAPTER FOURTEEN

When Kate and Deborah returned from Esporico, the luxury of Hotel Pitrizza was all the more pronounced. It was lovely coming back, like diving into a cool refreshing swimming pool after sweltering in the heat all day. Kat rushed to her villa, and lay back in the jacuzzi bath in the bathroom. Thankfully there was a mindless romantic comedy playin,g the sort of thing Kat loved when she needed to wind down.

Kat wanted to dress well for Bruno's send-off meal. Thankfully, she'd brought several fancy dresses with her in addition to her matron of honor dress, because Deborah had warned her Luigi loved to eat at fancy restaurants.

She picked out a jade green silk dress in a Grecian style. It had silver beaded detailing on the waist, and she spent a few minutes, looking at the jewelry she'd brought on the trip. She selected chandelier earrings with Swarovski crystals, a simple white gold snake chain for her neck, and a white gold bracelet watch Blaine had bought her a couple of birthdays ago. The watch looked so glamorous she didn't get to wear it much, but it was perfect with her outfit.

She had plenty of time before dinner, and Blaine was out somewhere with Luigi, so Kat took her time getting ready, and it felt sinfully decadent. The hotel bathroom cabinet was stocked to the brim with all kinds of beauty products, and Kat enjoyed looking at all of them, while wearing the white fluffy robe and slippers the hotel had provided. Eventually she picked out a "burnt sugar and ginger" body cream, and took her time massaging it in while still enjoying the mindless entertainment playing on the television.

Blaine came back just as she was fastening on her second chandelier earring, her outfit complete.

"Wow," he said. "Who's the glamorous movie star that I see before me?"

Kat grinned. "Oh, stop. I haven't even done my hair and makeup yet."

Blaine massaged her shoulders as she sat at the dressing table. "Well, I think you look perfect." He kissed her on top of the head. "How did it go in Esporico?"

"It was okay," Kat said. "We found out Bruno's brother is still in love with Chiari, and he'd just left to go up to the Lombardi estate. How was your day?"

"It was great," he said. "Luigi and I went sailing and had a man-to-man talk."

Kat smiled. "I'm glad you can be there to support him."

After Blaine changed into a gray linen suit, they made their way to the restaurant. It was a blend of traditional Italian stone, sleek, white, and luxurious, just like their villas. Luigi and Deborah were already seated at their table, drinking 1993 Dom Perignon. Luigi had a cigar in his mouth.

"We're going all out!" he said joyously to Kat and Blaine as they sat down at the table. He slapped Blaine on the back quite hard, and said, "Let's go wild for Bruno!"

And so they did, eating some of everything the hotel had prepared from focaccia bread to tiramisu and everything in between. Truly, the hotel kitchen staff had prepared a feast that would not soon be forgotten.

"Are you sure you should drink any more?" Deborah asked Luigi quietly as they were finishing dinner.

"Of course!" Luigi roared happily. "Bruno loved to drink and drink and drink and drink until the very last drop was gone. Good man, I say!" He poured more champagne into his glass until it was overflowing and spilled on the tablecloth. Then he lifted his glass in the air. "To Bruno!" he shouted in a loud voice.

Kat hadn't drunk quite as much, and consequently felt a little awkward about Luigi's boisterous conduct, but she couldn't hold it against him. This was his grieving process, after all. "I'll have another," she said, thrusting her glass out and trying to get in the spirit of things.

"Thatta girl!" Luigi said, and poured her a huge glass of champagne that spilled over the edge of her lass. But before long, his laughter turned to tears. "Bruno," he cried. "Where is Bruno? He should be here."

Other diners were looking over at their table, since Luigi was being quite loud. Kat glanced over at the staff. They hovered around, looking uncomfortable and feeling uncertain about what they should do. They couldn't very well ask Luigi to leave, since he was one of their best customers, and they knew he was mourning Bruno.

Kat saw one of the other diners go up to a staff member and point to their table. The staff member took the man and the woman he was with around a corner. It looked like the staff was going to move some of the other diners and let Luigi mourn in peace.

Deborah was holding Luigi close to her. "I know, my darling. You're right. He should be here."

Luigi wiped away his tears, and said, "Our wedding won't be the same without him."

Deborah looked worried. "Do you want to postpone the wedding, out of respect for Bruno?"

"No, definitely not," Luigi said. Suddenly his voice sounded much less slurred. "Bruno would have hated me to do that. He was so happy I was marrying you and had found a true love. He wouldn't want us to postpone that for even a moment. And he will be there in spirit, cheering us on. Then I will have two best men. One in the spirit, one with us."

"Have you decided who you're going to have as your best man?" Kat asked.

"No, I haven't," Luigi said. "But it will be a good man. A man Bruno would have approved of."

CHAPTER FIFTEEN

The next morning they returned to the Lombardi estate. Kat and Deborah were hoping to see Salvatore. They were disappointed, and very surprised, to learn that he and Chiari had decided to go out for the day.

They were sitting on the veranda with Primo, trying to work out how to politely refuse the copious cakes and alcohol Chiari's family kept trying to force on them, while Luigi and Blaine went for a walk through the vineyards.

Kat said, "Chiari and Salvatore are really not making themselves look good, are they?"

"They're innocent, that's why," Deborah answered. "It would be more suspicious if things were awkward between them."

"Hmm." Kat sipped on some more of her Guappa. It seemed to be Chiari's family's favorite, and looked out at the glittering Mediterranean. "I don't know."

"So, what?" Deborah said, in an incredulous tone of voice. "You think the two of them teamed up to get rid of Bruno, so they both could inherit the estate and live happily ever after? Chiari found out Bruno was cheating and reverted back to how she felt about Salvatore before she married Bruno, even after all these years?"

"I've heard of crazier things," Kat said.

"And now, with Bruno not yet in the ground, they're out on a date." Deborah gave her a slightly withering look. "No, I would bet that they're out making funeral arrangements. The two of them were his closest relatives."

"Maybe, maybe not."

Deborah sighed. "This whole thing is beginning to totally stress me out. I don't know how you do it."

Kat found a smile from somewhere. "Yes, it is very stressful, and I know what you mean. In fact, it's so stressful, and there's so much at stake, that sometimes I just have to numb out. Like if I were to allow myself to shoulder all that pressure, I'd just crumble, so I have to find a place of deep calm within myself. I step back, and try to look at everything objectively."

"That's a real skill, wish I could do it."

"I think it comes from being a writer," said Kat. "I can kind of 'step out' of the scene and take a bird's eye view of it. It also stops me from jumping to conclusions. Books take all sorts of unexpected twists and turns before you arrive at the ending. And, as they say, life is stranger than fiction."

"That's really something, Kat."

"Well, we all have our skills, Deborah. I couldn't do what you do. For one, I couldn't teach. For another, I'd just about die talking about sex in public. Sure, I can write about it behind the safety of my pen name, Sexy Cissy." She laughed. "But that's about it."

"When you've been talking about it every day for the past fifteen years as I've been doing in the classes I teach, it becomes second nature," Deborah said with a chuckle.

"That's what I hope happens with my writing," Kat said ruefully.

"I wish I could just see an empty page, and it would all start flowing from my fingertips without any thought. Unfortunately, it takes a great deal of mental energy."

"I can imagine," Deborah said.

"But the sense of satisfaction is unreal. When I finally type out 'the end', I get a high that can last for days. I guess that's another similarity with investigating. Both writing and investigating have a very clear end moment. You come to the end of one, and then you move onto the next."

"The next?" Deborah asked with a smile. "You mean you're planning to do more investigating? Are you going to become Lindsay's answer to Miss Marple? Although a much more glamorous Miss Marple, I might add."

Kat gave her a playful swipe. "And a heck of a lot younger, thank you very much." She looked out over the vineyards. "Well to answer your question, no, I'm not hoping another Lindsay resident drops dead so I can whip out my magnifying glass, but I'll certainly be there if I'm needed."

"Maybe you should start your own private investigating firm!"

Kat laughed. "No thanks. First of all, Blaine would go crazy. He'd be worried sick all the time. I don't think his nerves could take it."

"That's a valid point," Deborah said. "I couldn't live with someone who was employed in a dangerous line of work, either."

"I suppose it wouldn't be a barrel of laughs, would it?" Kat asked. "Sitting at home every night wondering if you're going to get the call you've always been dreading, or if a police officer is going show up at your door with bad news."

Deborah shuddered. "The whole thing sounds awful."

"It certainly does," Kat said in agreement as she looked at her watch. "I wonder when the vineyard manager will get here. He's got a very glamorous name, hasn't he? Gabriele Ferrari."

"He does to our American ears," Deborah agreed. "So many Italian names sound glamorous to us, but I've learned they don't sound glamorous to other Italians."

Kat laughed. "I guess. It's like that old joke about Enrique Iglesias. Sounds wonderful in Spanish, but Henry Churches doesn't sound so exciting, does it?"

"Oh, I've never heard that before!" Deborah said. "That's brilliant."

Eventually Gabriele, the vineyard manager, arrived. Luigi had let him know earlier that Kat and Deborah wanted to speak with him, but he'd taken his own sweet time coming to see them.

"Hello," he said in English when he arrived on the veranda. He gave them a professional smile and handshake, neither of which seemed to be sincere or warm. Kat took an instant dislike to him, but tried to keep an open mind.

Primo sat at Deborah's feet and glared at him.

He sat down and sneered at what was sitting on the table in a glass pitcher. "Why do they bring Guappa when there is some of the world's best wine here to drink?" He looked at their glasses and raised his eyebrows. "Oh, sorry." Then he arranged his face into a smile. "How can I help you lovely ladies? I am sorry I took a little longer than expected to get here. We are rushing the new release through."

"The new release?" Kat said, astounded. "The same one Bruno was trying when he was murdered?"

"Unfortunately, we have to," Gabriele said. "We've invested a huge amount of time and money this year for this release. If we don't release it, we will incur a significant loss. That would not be beneficial to whoever inherits the estate from Mr. Lombardi."

Kat couldn't help but think he was a rather cold type of individual. "Did you and Mr. Lombardi usually agree on the work involved in the vineyards and the wine production?"

"Of course," Gabriele said. "I worked for him for ten years. Mr. Lombardi was the kind of man who would fire you if you exhibited anything less than excellence." He sat up very straight with a superior look on his face. He left a long silence, speaking without words, letting them know how excellent he obviously was.

"Who had access to the cellar?" Kat asked.

"Me, and some of the workers in the vineyard. None of them would have any motive to kill Mr. Lombardi, and I certainly don't. I'm confident my position as the vineyard manager is not in jeopardy. Believe me, the profit alone from this successful upcoming release will guarantee that, but vineyard workers are expendable. Any of them could be fired, for any reason, at any time. None of them stand to gain anything from Mr. Lombardi's death."

"I see," Kat said. She poured more Guappa to give herself some time to think. She did so very slowly, pondering whether what Gabriele said was true or not. Did he really not stand to gain from Bruno's death? She couldn't think of any real motive that he'd have, but perhaps he was acting on behalf of some other winemaker. Maybe he'd been recruited by one of them to take a job at the Lombardi estate so he could eventually kill Bruno. But waiting ten years to get rid of someone would be an awfully long-term strategy. She couldn't see that happening. Still, she asked, "Who were you employed by before you started to work here?"

"I was a wine expert for one of the most famous international wine magazines. I was not a vineyard manager, but Mr. Lombardi would not let me continue to waste my talent, so he said, when we met at an event. I allowed him to, shall we say, poach me. I relocated my young family from Venice and came here."

Deborah and Kat exchanged glances. The way he spoke was so mechanical and devoid of emotion it was quite chilling.

Kat took a deep breath. "I hope you don't find this to be a rude question, Mr. Ferrari," she said, "but you don't seem to be that disturbed by Mr. Lombardi's death."

He looked her straight in the eye, a look that pierced into her very core, so piercing she had to look away. "Not all of humanity wears their hearts on their sleeves, madam," he said. "Not everything is as it appears. Not in the wine world. Neither in the wider world. If you opt to judge by appearances, you will make many errors."

Kat sighed. There was something about the man's manner that sucked the will to live out of her. She felt depressed and flat and momentarily thought about packing this all up and going back home to Lindsay, but she knew she couldn't. Wearily, she asked, "So, do you have any idea who might have killed Bruno Lombardi?"

"I am neither a detective nor an investigator," he said drily. "But I can tell you that many in the wine community envied Mr. Lombardi. Those who do not have the will or skill to reach the very peak of excellence always envy those who have the disposition, talent, and discipline to achieve it."

"Are you speaking about anyone in particular?" Deborah asked, barely able to conceal the irritation in her voice.

"Well, if you've done even half a job, you'll already know that there was certainly no love lost between the winemaker, Vito Rizzo, and Mr. Lombardi."

"Thank you," Kat said, and made a mental note of the name.

"You mean to tell me you did not even know that? Well, Luigi obviously has some sort of faith in you. I hope he is right."

Kat couldn't wait to get away from this odious man, but she still had questions. "Let's say Vito Rizzo killed Bruno…"

"I never said such a thing," Gabriele interrupted.

"I'm not saying that you did," Kat snapped back. "Now, hear me out. Hypothetically, say Rizzo was the one who was responsible for Bruno's death. Who would have done it? Who would have had access to the cellar? Would one of the workers in the vineyard have taken payment from Rizzo to sneak into the cellar and add poison to the wine?" She wanted to add, "Or would you?" but she didn't want to jeopardize the interview.

He shook his head. "I told you that I am not an investigator. I make excellent wine. And the thing about excellence is to know your sphere, and to only operate within that sphere. Therefore, I have nothing to say."

"But you don't need to be an expert in this," Kat said. "A man off the street could tell you that was plausible. What I'm asking is, in your position as vineyard manager, do you think that could have been possible?"

He stood up and spoke tightly. "My time and attention must be focused on this new release. I cannot sit around all day musing about murder motives. I know my place as an excellent winemaker and vineyard manager, not as a half-rate policeman."

Kat wondered if that was a dig at her. In any case, it didn't really matter, because she couldn't imagine disliking him more than she already did.

"You've made yourself very clear," Kat said. "Thank you for your time."

"You're welcome," he said, practically through gritted teeth. He walked back into the mansion with a stiffer gait than when he'd walked onto the veranda earlier.

Deborah looked at Kat, totally bewildered. "What was that all about?"

"You know as much as I do," Kat said. "That's a very strange man."

"You've got that right. We should keep an eye on him."

Kat thought for a moment. "I think you're right. After all, he's the one who would have had the easiest time slipping the poison into the bottle. The only problem is, I don't see a motive."

Deborah shivered. "People like that don't need a motive. From what I've read, people like that kill for fun. Did you see the look in his eyes? Scary."

"They were rather piercing, weren't they?" Kat answered in agreement.

CHAPTER SIXTEEN

For lunch, Kat, Deborah, Blaine, and Luigi were treated to a lovely spaghetti bolognaise, courtesy of one of Chiari's cousins. Well, actually, Kat learned that spaghetti bolognaise doesn't exist in Italy. Instead, it was *tagliatelle al ragù,* with thick tagliatelle instead of spaghetti. It was absolutely delicious, and clearly laced with copious amounts of red wine. Kat could taste it in the sauce. Primo got a whole bowl of it himself, and wolfed it down at lightning speed.

Over lunch, Kat tried to shake off the weird, uncomfortable feeling Gabriele had left her with. He'd made her feel very uneasy, and she was finding it difficult to get rid of the feeling.

"Are you okay, darling?" Blaine asked her quietly when Deborah and Luigi returned the dishes to the kitchen.

"I think so," she said. "I just have this awful feeling of dread. Like something terrible is going to happen."

Blaine frowned. "Something like what?"

"I don't know," said Kat. "That's the thing. I just feel... ugh. It's horrible."

Blaine wrapped her up in a hug. "Well, nothing terrible is going to happen to you with me here."

"The sooner I wrap up this investigation, the better," Kat said. She felt all the more determined to make something happen, to get to the bottom of things. Impatience pumped through her. She hadn't found out anything yet. At least, that was how it felt.

After lunch, Luigi and Blaine left for a round of golf at the exclusive Pevero Golf Club where Luigi was a member. Blaine asked Kat if she'd rather he didn't go, given how she was feeling. She smiled at him and told him to have a great round of golf.

As soon as they were out the door, she turned to Deborah. "We've got to get serious. Let's go and find this mistress of Bruno's. Her name's Sofia Ossani, isn't it?"

Deborah nodded. "I think that's what Chiari said."

Kat already had the rental car keys in her hand. "Let's hit the road. Of course it might help if we knew where she lived. I wonder how we can find out. Maybe there was a postmark on the letter the son sent." They called Chiari, who was still out with Salvatore, something Kat definitely wanted to speak to her about, and she gave them the name of the town where Sofia lived. She didn't know the exact address, but that didn't matter. It was a very small town and everyone knew everyone.

When they were in the rental car, Primo secured in the back, Deborah punched the name of the town into the GPS.

"Oh, dear," Kat said as she looked at the GPS. It was a three hour drive, all the way to the end of the island. The little seaside village where Salvatore lived was on the way. "We're really going to rack up the miles, plus we won't get back until late this evening." She paused for a moment. "We also have to go see Vito Rizzo. Do you know where he lives?"

"He's in the south of the island as well," Deborah said. "Luigi mentions him from time to time, and not in glowing terms. I'm not looking forward to that visit."

"Do you think it would be a better use of our time to stay down there for the night? We could ask Luigi and Blaine if they'd join us after their golf."

Deborah smiled. "Sounds like a plan. I'll give Luigi a call."

Soon they'd agreed to meet at a lovely resort hotel near the south end of the island. Before long, Kat was driving the rental car out of the driveway and through the expansive vineyards, ready to make that now-familiar journey down the coast.

They chatted about everything and nothing on the drive to the south end of the island, that is, everything except the investigation. They spoke about Lacie and Tyler, and about Kat's books. They giggled like schoolgirls about Kat's sexy new book release. Then Deborah spoke about her new discovery, Brené Brown, a researcher who gave talks on all kinds of interesting topics, such as the power of vulnerability. Deborah wasn't usually into self-help, she said, but Brené Brown based all her work on good solid data. Kat made a mental note to look her up.

They talked about Deborah's job, Primo, and the workings of vineyards, until they were both thoroughly tired from talking. They turned on the radio, and Kat found a jazz station. It felt very relaxing cruising down the coast with soft jazz filling the car.

"Oh, look," Deborah said, pointing to a sign. "There's the turn for the town."

Kat followed the signs to the little town where Sofia lived. It was quite a ways in from the coast, nestled among mountains. Everyone stared at them when they entered the town, the people apparently not used to seeing outsiders. Small stone houses climbed up the sides of a nearby mountain, and the little town as a whole presented a very picturesque scene.

Kat slowed the car down so Deborah could speak to an older man in Italian and ask him where Sofia lived. "It's the largest stone house up on the mountain," Deborah told Kat. "The man I asked said we can't miss it. It has large golden gates."

"That sounds fancy," Kat said, and followed Deborah's directions up a winding mountain road. Soon they came to the golden gates, which were thankfully open. Kat felt a little intrusive just driving right into the driveway, but she did.

The front door opened and a buxom blonde woman with curlers in her hair and her face heavily made up appeared, a frown on her face. "Who are you?" she asked in Italian.

Deborah explained in Italian that she was Luigi's friend, and Kat was her friend. She asked the woman if she was Sofia Ossani.

Yes," Sofia said. Deborah told her they would like to talk to her for a few minutes about Bruno Lombardi. Sofia motioned for them to come inside, and looked around the neighborhood with a worried look on her face as she let them in. She also looked worriedly at Primo.

Deborah reassured her in Italian about Primo and put a leash on him. Sofia still looked worried, but nodded, and Primo came in with them.

She led them into the living room. A young dark-haired boy was playing on a gamin console with a grown man, also blond. The boy didn't even look up. The grown man offered them a quick smile, then went back to the virtual soccer game he and the boy were playing. Sofia rolled her eyes at them and began making coffee.

Whenever Sofia or Kat spoke, Deborah translated.

"What is it about Bruno that you want to talk to me about?" Sofia asked.

"First, I just wanted to say how sorry we are about Bruno," Kat said.

Sofia frowned. "Sorry about him? Sorry about what?"

Kat and Deborah looked at each other in alarm.

"She doesn't know," Kat said in English to Deborah.

Deborah had the unenviable job of breaking the news of Bruno's death to Sofia. She gasped, and the boy, who had overheard the conversation, froze.

"No," she said, shaking her head again and again. "No. No. No." Then she broke down in tears.

The man tried to put his arm around the boy, but the boy struck out at him, punching him in the stomach.

"Papa!" he shouted, then ran to Sofia and buried his head in her chest, like a much younger child would do.

Kat remembered the note the boy had written. Diego was his name she recalled. He was now sobbing, and his mother was crying as well.

Kat and Deborah sat, watching the scene. Kat's heart broke for both of them, despite the adultery. It was obvious they clearly had adored Bruno, and Diego was faced with having to deal with the loss of his father.

"I am Rinaldo Ossani," the man said in Italian. Again Deborah had to translate. "Sofia is my sister. I have been telling her that she should end her relationship with Bruno, because he was taking her for a fool. But in death, I suppose none of that matters."

Kat nodded. "Death does change things. We forgive more quickly."

"Yes," he said. "When he was alive, I had nothing good to say about him. Now?" He choked. "He had some good points, I can see that now."

"Did you know him?" Kat asked.

"I worked for him until just recently," Rinaldo said. "I was fired because of the horrible vineyard manager."

Kat looked wide-eyed at Deborah and said. "Yes, Gabriele is not the most pleasant person in the world."

Rinaldo swore. "I would not be surprised if he killed Bruno. The man is a psychopath."

Kat leaned forward in her chair. "Why would you say that? What reason would he have to kill Bruno?"

"He always wanted to be at the forefront of everything. Ever since his days at the magazine, he has courted publicity. He loves fame. Adores the limelight. But so does, or actually I should say, so did Bruno. Bruno never allowed Gabriele to have his face on the labels of the bottles, or conduct interviews, or make any appearances. Bruno kept him firmly behind the scenes, and he hated it. The way he saw it, he did all the hard work, and Bruno just milked all the glory. He was very resentful about it."

Kat's heart was beating more quickly. "Bruno was poisoned. The poison was left in a wine bottle in the cellar."

"That makes sense," Rinaldo said. "He could easily slip the poison into the bottle. Other people have access to the cellar, but Gabriele tries to keep all of them out. He thinks it's his domain. As a matter of fact, he thinks the whole place is his domain."

"So you think Gabriele could have possibly killed Bruno, so that he could get in the limelight?"

"I do not know, but it seems likely," Rinaldo said. "Of course, Chiari will inherit the whole estate…"

"What about my son?" Sofia asked in a loud voice, wiping her tears as her sadness turned to anger. "He will not be cast aside!"

"Who are you kidding?" Rinaldo shouted at her. "Bruno cast him aside in life, and he will cast him aside in death, too. He never publicly acknowledged him. Don't be so stupid."

Sofia continued to sob.

"Sorry for my temper," Rinaldo said. "Sofia is just stupid enough to believe that Bruno would leave Chiari for her or her son, when it was never going to happen. Not in life, not in death. Chiari will inherit the whole estate. She is not interested in wine. She will hand over the winemaking process to Gabriele. He will finally get all the glory, just like he so desperately craves."

Kat blew a stream of air out of her lips. "It's definitely a theory."

"It is," he said. "The only other person I could think of who would want to kill Bruno is Vito Rizzo."

Kat's eyes widened. "His name keeps coming up."

"For good reason," Rinaldo said. "He hates Bruno with all his heart and soul."

"But how could he have managed to get the poison into the wine bottle?"

Rinaldo shrugged. "Maybe he and Gabriele are in it together. No, Gabriele would not want to share the glory again, and Rizzo would probably be intimidated by him. Maybe one of the vineyard workers was paid off by him."

"Yes, I'd thought of that," Kat said. "Can you give me a list of names? I will be interviewing them eventually."

Rinaldo wrote the names of his former colleagues down on the back of an envelope and handed the list to Kat. "These were the ones below me, which means they wouldn't have access to a key. But the names of these people," he drew stars by some of them, "are in more of a supervisory capacity. They will have keys."

Kat folded the envelope and tucked it in her purse. "Thank you, Rinaldo."

Diego was now snuggled into his mother's lap. He turned to face Kat and Deborah and looked at them with hateful eyes. He said something in Italian.

Deborah rocked back, shocked, then turned to Kat. "He said he hates us because his father is dead."

"Talk about shoot the messenger," Kat said, then lowered her voice a little, even though no one in their company could speak English. "Is he... okay? In the letter he sent, and now, he seems very..." She couldn't think of the right word.

"He's a very angry young man, for sure," Deborah said.

"Yes," Kat agreed.

Sofia had resumed crying uncontrollably.

"Maybe we should leave them to grieve for a while," said Kat, and come back tomorrow? It seems awful to ask them a load of questions when they're in this state."

"You're right," said Deborah.

They said their goodbyes and condolences, and left.

CHAPTER SEVENTEEN

After they left Sofia, Kat and Deborah decided to check into the hotel where Luigi had arranged for them to stay. It was a beautiful luxury boutique hotel in the city center of Cagliari, Sardinia's capital. Luigi had called ahead and insisted that Primo be allowed to stay there, indicating he would pay a heavy premium if necessary. Kat loved driving through the city, with all its historic, brightly-colored buildings. They eventually pulled up outside the hotel, which had a muted red and gold exterior reaching up four floors.

The inside was no disappointment, and their room was old-style Italian plush. After a quick hot shower, though, they were at a loss for what to do. They got a text from Luigi saying he and Blaine were running late and wouldn't make it for dinner. The men would grab dinner on the road, and they urged the women to treat themselves.

"Why don't we pay a visit to the much-talked-about Mr. Rizzo?" Kat said.

Deborah sighed. "Oh, gosh, now that I've heard so much about him, I'm dreading it."

"Me too, a little," said Kat. "But I don't think anyone could be worse than Gabriele."

They needn't have worried. They caught Vito Rizzo in his

absolute element. They looked him up online to find the address of his winery. He had a tasting room open to the public. When they got there, it was swarming with locals and tourists.

Rizzo had a cigar on an ashtray that he kept picking up and putting down. He was pouring wine himself, and smiling and laughing with the patrons. He had a loud, booming voice that carried across the room, but Kat could tell he was the type of guy who would be just as loud when he was mad.

She decided to play it differently. She got in line and eventually sauntered up to him with an empty glass. "Hello," she said in English.

"Hello." He replied in English with a wide smile and thick Italian accent. "Welcome to Rizzo's winery. I hope you will enjoy yourself immensely."

She smiled as he poured. "I expect to. Your wine was recommended to me by some very good friends. I understand it's the best in Sardinia."

"You understand correctly," he said. "Though not everyone does. Someone else usually gets that award."

"Oh, who's that?" Kat asked, sipping her wine innocently.

"Bruno Lombardi, of course."

"Oh, yes."

"Though now that he's dead, maybe I have a chance to be number one." He laughed very loudly. "Sorry, that was in bad taste, wasn't it?"

"Perhaps," Kat said. She looked at him over the top of her glass. "I think you should know that I'm investigating Bruno Lombardi's murder."

The smile fell from Vito's face, and all the color drained out of it. "Come into the back with me now," he said in a commanding voice.

"I would be happy to." Kat signaled to Deborah, and they both followed Vito out of the crowded room and into a nearby office.

He sat down behind a large desk and motioned for the two of them to sit down. He was so panicked he didn't even greet Deborah or ask Kat her name. "Are you with the police? No, you can't be. You must be some kind of private investigation team?"

"Something like that," Kat said evenly.

"Please, please," he said, "do not get me wrong. I did not like Mr. Lombardi. He was my professional rival. I joke about him, but I did not kill him. I am not a murderer."

Kat watched him, hoping he would blurt out more in his panic.

"It's okay, it's okay," he said, seemingly more to himself than to them. "I have an alibi." He took out his cell phone. "Look. I know the date and time he was killed. Everyone in the wine industry knows about it. At that time I was at a wedding shower here in the winery. A couple from one of the local villages decided to hold their shower here." He flicked through several photographs shown on the screen of his cell phone and stopped at one particular photograph.

"Look. Here's one of me with the happy couple." He clicked a little icon, a circle with the letter 'I' inside. "Look at the time. 7:05 p.m. I was here. That's the time he was killed, right?"

"Yes, 7:00 p.m.," Kat said. "You certainly do have an alibi. You could not have committed the murder."

Vito looked exceptionally relieved. He even began to smile again.

"While you could not have committed the murder personally," Kat said. "and I'm not accusing you, only looking at every possibility. Is it not possible you could have ordered him to be killed?"

Vito lost his smile immediately. "Yes. It is possible."

Kat's heart started beating. Was that a confession? Would solving the murder be that easy? She glanced at Deborah, who was gripping the edges of her chair a little too tightly.

"But I did not," Vito said. "Listen, if I had wanted to win this wine war by unfair means, I would have done so a long time ago, but I refuse to stoop to that level. I can only struggle to convince the critics that my wine is the best. Bruno is… was an excellent showman. He was something akin to a celebrity.

"I had to build my own celebrity brand to counter him, but I am not lean and muscular with big brown eyes. Nevertheless, I was working on, and am still working on, an old Italian grandfather style of marketing." He leaned forward. "Now, do you have any more questions?"

The abruptness with which he switched topics threw Kat off. Perhaps it was designed to, but she had no way of knowing. All she knew was that her mind was blank. "Hang on a second."

He stood up. "I don't have a second. Part of my branding is that I am always present. That I am accessible. I need to be outside, serving wine."

"But…"

"In any case, I am not obliged to answer any of your questions. You are not the police." He handed them a business card from a holder on his desk. "If you have any further questions, please direct them to my publicist."

"That's not exactly accessible!" said Deborah.

He was losing patience. "Accessible to paying customers, not to people poking around my business."

"We're not poking," Kat said. "We're…"

"I don't have time for this!" he bellowed.

Kat stood up, her adrenaline pumping. "You have to have time for this! You're making yourself look very suspicious, Mr. Rizzo. If you were innocent, I would think you would jump at the chance to clear your name."

"What else can I tell you?" he shot back. "I showed you where I was at the time of the murder. Then you accuse me of paying someone else to do it. I've already told you that is not the case. What more do you want from me?"

In all honesty, Kat just wanted a meandering conversation. One where she could scope him out and explore any issues that came up. She couldn't think of a plausible answer to his question.

"Thank you for your visit," Vito said insincerely with a fake smile on his face. "Hope you can come by Rizzo winery any time, to enjoy the wine."

He ushered them out the door. Kat's head was in such a whirl, she couldn't think of what to say to change his mind. He was a very strange character. *Very temperamental*, she thought.

Before they really knew what had happened, she and Deborah were outside in the parking lot, blinking in the late afternoon sunlight. They made their way back to the car to get some shade.

"Well," Kat said, sitting behind the steering wheel. "That certainly wasn't productive."

"It wasn't too bad," said Deborah. "At least we know he didn't commit the murder himself."

"Yeah, but I wouldn't have expected him to," Kat said. "Can't imagine him creeping into a cellar unnoticed, can you?"

Deborah suppressed a laugh. "Perhaps not."

"It is possible he could have paid one of the vineyard workers to do it, if he's in cahoots with them? When we get back to the Lombardi estate, we can check up on the workers, and see if any of them know him personally."

"That sounds like a good plan."

Kat pulled the car out of the parking lot. "I've had enough of difficult men for one day, between Gabriele and Vito Rizzo. I say let's go back to the hotel, get room service, and watch a mindless movie."

Deborah smiled. "That sounds like an excellent plan."

*****

Even though she'd had a shower earlier, Kat took a long soak in the tub while they waited for their dinner to arrive. After all that driving, her body was telling her that she needed it. They'd agreed that Deborah would do the driving the next day.

She lay back in the bubbles and thought about each of the suspects. Rizzo could have hired someone to put the poison in the wine bottle. Gabriele could have done it too, for his own reasons. Even Chiari could have done it, as an act of revenge. Sofia could have, too, for the same reason. What about Rinaldo? Perhaps he was angry about being fired, and decided to seek his own revenge.

Kat's mind boggled. There were just too many possibilities.

She tried to think of other things. She texted a message to Lacie on WhatsApp. Lacie had sent her pictures of Jazz and Rudy enjoying themselves on their long dog walks and anther picture of them curled up on the couch with Tyler and her. Kat replied saying how happy they all looked. Her heart felt warm seeing the pictures. She missed them all, even though she'd only been gone a short time. She missed Lindsay, too. She didn't know how Deborah had done it – uprooting her whole life to move to a foreign country. Kat was certainly enjoying the trip, but she'd enjoy going back home, too.

She padded back into her room (they'd gotten two, but Deborah had come over from hers to join Kat for the evening) to find Deborah doing a soduku puzzle and looking at the Hugh Grant romcom now and then, with Primo curled up at her feet. The décor of the room was rich and sumptuous, with reds and purples and brown leather furniture. Deborah had drawn the heavy red curtains and the room was bathed in soft golden lamplight. It looked and felt unbelievably cozy.

It only got better when their dinner arrived. They'd gone for real comfort food, to make up for the difficult day they'd had. Kat had ordered pizza. "I can't believe I've had so little pizza so far. I'm in Italy, for goodness' sake!" she'd said before ordering. She'd gone for a sundried tomato, olive, oregano, and pulled pork pizza.

Deborah had chosen lasagna. For their side dishes, they'd chosen a green salad and a plateful of *arancini* – little golden brown balls filled with rice, tomato sauce and mozzarella. Then to finish, they'd both chosen *gelato.* Kat went for *nicciola,* which was hazelnut, while Deborah opted for *zuppa ingelese.* "That translates to English soup," Deborah had said, laughing. "No idea what it is, but I'll try it."

They began to eat their main dish and sides, and before they knew what had happened, it was all gone.

"Time to try the English soup," Deborah said. She dipped her spoon in the *gelato* and tasted it. "Oh, it tastes like custard!" Deborah had been to England many times. "Wow. They sure are creative. Now I can see why they named it that."

Kat and Deborah were happy to spend their evening watching the movie. They were both tired from their emotionally draining day, and both of them ended up falling asleep before the movie had finished, Deborah in the armchair, and Kat on top of the bed quilt.

They didn't wake up until Luigi and Blaine came in. Kat was still only half awake, since they'd been very quiet when they'd come in. She was just happy to get under the covers in the dim-light, feeling full and warm and safe, and then to cuddle up to Blaine and fall into a deep, restful sleep. Talk about golf and their detective work would have to wait until the following morning.

CHAPTER EIGHTEEN

The next morning, the four of them decided to take it easy. The previous day had been a long day for all of them, so Kat and Blaine were perfectly happy to have a light breakfast in their room, and then take a lazy morning walk through Cagliari.

In the medieval quarter, with its limestone walls and rustic charm, they found a little restaurant that smelled so delicious they decided to stop there for lunch. They called Deborah and Luigi and asked them to join them. They enjoyed a glass of wine while they waited for them. It was a sunny day with a gentle breeze blowing, and Kat could feel the stress from the previous day melt away.

When Deborah and Luigi arrived with Primo, they looked much more relaxed, too. They talked about things that had nothing to do with Bruno or his murder, but instead chatted about the cultural differences between the United States and Italy, where they'd traveled before, and places that were on their wish list.

Kat had a delicious dish of spaghetti, wild asparagus wrapped in pancetta, and *bottarga,* salted fish eggs. Blaine had chargrilled sardines with capers and *bruschetta.* Deborah opted for pasta shells with walnuts, clams, chili and *bottarga,* while Luigi had pan-fried seabass with a cannellini bean mash. As is always the case, all good things have to come to an end sometime, and soon their investigation-free bliss came to an end. Kat began to start thinking about what they'd do next.

"Deborah," she said. "I think we should go back to Sofia's and ask her some more questions. She's had time for the news of Bruno's death to sink in by now." She turned to Luigi and Blaine. "She didn't even know Bruno had died. We had to break the news to her."

"That doesn't surprise me," Luigi said. "Unless she's in the wine community, she would not know. The local press here in the south part of the island seldom report events such as murders that occur in the northern part of the island. It's just not newsworthy, so I'm not surprised she didn't know about Bruno's death. By the way, Chiari called to say the police are doing some investigating up there, and seem to be zeroing in on Bruno's brother Salvatore. She's very upset about it.

"She also told me that the police have positively confirmed that Bruno died from drinking poison that had been put in the bottle of wine he was drinking."

Kat nodded. "He does seem to have some powerful motives, but powerful motives don't always lead to murder. I'm keeping an open mind."

"That's the best way," Luigi agreed.

"Luigi, I'd like to go ocean fishing," Blaine said. "Do you have any interest in doing that? I think we should leave these investigators alone so they can do their job."

"Good idea," Luigi said.

"Kat, give me a call if you find out anything, would you?" Blaine asked, then he said with a smile, "Even though I know you can handle whatever comes up, it will make me feel better."

"Thanks for the vote of confidence, darling," Kat said, giving him a kiss on the cheek. "See you later."

Kat, Deborah, and Primo returned to the hotel and got the valet to bring their rental car around. Deborah drove. The drive up to the little town where Sofia lived was lovely. It was a warm day, with the sun shining brightly, but a wonderful Mediterranean breeze took the edge off the heat. They turned off the air-conditioner and opened the windows. Kat felt like if the murder didn't exist, she'd be in paradise.

"Sounds like the police are closing in on Salvatore, don't you agree?" Deborah asked.

"Seems like they are," Kat said, "but I don't think he did it."

"Why not?"

"Well, from what Alessa said, he sounded quite depressed, didn't he? He was in that small, rundown seaside town, where life is very slow. He wasn't motivated to put work into the B and B, she did that, and he basically spent his life talking about the past. He was still in love with Chiari, despite all the time that's gone by.

"I don't know how to explain what I feel, but it sounds like he was stuck in a rut. Maybe that's the best way to describe him. Alessa said his depression was quite severe. I just don't think there's enough, let's call it movement, for him to commit a murder. It seems to me he wouldn't have the capability to do it. I mean, he would have the intelligence, but would he have the drive? He seemed to have turned into a kind of character where a life-changing eventhappened to him in the past, rather than him making anything happen in his present-day life."

"Hmm, I see what you mean," Deborah said. "That's quite insightful, Kat. I'm impressed. Perhaps you're right. Alessa was certainly calling the shots at the B and B. Then again, oh, I don't know."

"Go on."

"Maybe it all finally became too much for him and he snapped," Deborah said.

"Hmm... Maybe," Kat said. She thought about it for a moment. "But I don't think so. I mean, people who snap tend to stab or strangle when they kill someone. Poisoning is too calculated. It takes too long to coordinate. If the killer just snapped, half way through organizing how to administer the poison, they'd have backed out."

"Yes, I think you're right about that," Deborah said. "Good point."

Primo barked happily in the back as if to say, "You're right, Kat."

They soon arrived at the small town where Sofia lived, and drove up the mountain road toward her home. The gates were closed this time, but there was a smaller gate to the side where a person could walk through, and it was open. Deborah parked the car a short distance down the street. They couldn't park any closer because there was a hairpin curve in the road just a bit further up the hill, and parking outside Sofia's house might have led to their car being hit if another car came down the hill too fast.

Deborah got out the car and put a leash on Primo. Primo was unusually energetic. He kept looking up at the house and growling. "Stop that, Primo," Deborah said gently, ruffling him under the neck. "You'll scare them so much they won't allow you to go in the house."

As they walked toward Sofia's house, Kat tried to think of questions she'd like to ask Sofia. Usually she just did it on the fly, but she had so many mixed emotions about Sofia and Diego that she felt blocked. She didn't know whether to judge Sofia or feel sorry for her, or both, and it was quite distracting.

When they arrived at the small gate they heard a man and a woman shouting angrily at each other through an open downstairs window, but they weren't close enough to understand what was being said.

Kat and Deborah exchanged a look.

"Let's get closer," Kat said quietly. "Don't alert them or let them see us. I want to hear this."

They crept closer, edging up against a bougainvillea plant, trying to keep out of view from the window. They couldn't look in the window or they'd risk being spotted.

"I'm sure that's Sofia and her brother," Deborah whispered, listening to the voices.

"I agree," Kat said. They were getting close enough to hear the what they were saying, but even so, they still only caught a few words here and there. "Do you understand what they're saying?"

"No," Deborah whispered. "We need to get a little closer." She shot Primo a warning look and put her finger to her lips. "Shh!"

They crouched down and crept closer and closer, until they were standing immediately next to the side of the window. The sash window was very large and fully open at the bottom. Kat was thankful Sofia didn't have a gravel driveway. They managed to creep up to the window walking on a concrete surface, so they made no sound.

Deborah nodded to Kat to indicate she could understand what was being said. Then her eyes widened. She listened, then whispered frantic translations to Kat.

"She's saying, 'Bruno was the love of my life. Now I will never be his wife, and Diego will never be the master of the vineyard, as he promised.'"

Rinaldo screamed at her.

Deborah whispered, "He says… 'You were never going to be his wife, anyway, he didn't love you! You were just his kept woman, and the kid was nothing more than an unfortunate accident.'"

They heard the short, sharp cracking sound of a slap, which they assumed must be Sofia slapping Rinaldo.

Deborah translated, "He says... 'You're pathetic. You can slap me all you want, but it does not mean that what I am saying is not true. You know I am not lying. Bruno was always going to stay with his wife. Don't you know who she was? From a very prominent family in Lazio?

"Furthermore, don't you know who you are? People like you and me don't marry rich people like Bruno and live the life he and his wife did. No, we're just the hired help. You were a maid until you got knocked up, and I was someone who worked in the vineyard. That's as good as it gets for people like us.'"

"She just said, 'But I loved him. I still love him,'" Deborah translated.

Kat heard Sofia's strangled sob coming from deep in her throat.

Deborah said, "He's saying... 'You're stupid. Totally and utterly stupid to believe in such fairytales.'"

Kat held her breath.

Deborah's eyes practically popped out of her head. "She just said, 'You shouldn't have done it.'"

Kat gasped. "Done what?"

Rinaldo spoke again, and Deborah said with alarm, "He said, 'I poisoned him for you and my nephew. Maybe now you can find someone who really loves you.'"

"How could you poison him?"

"It was easy. I knew when he was going to try the new release. All I had to do was wait until Gabriele left. There was always a little time between the two. It was dusk, so no one saw me. I still had the key to the wine cellar."

Kat gasped. "Oh no."

At those words, Sofia went into a rage. Her voice was barely comprehensible, because she was screaming so loudly.

"She's saying, 'How could you? How could you? How could you kill my love?'" Deborah said. "'I should kill you!'"

Kat heard the terror in Rinaldo's voice as he said, "No, Sofia, no!" Kat had to see what was going on. She stood up, and saw a gun in Sofia's shaking hand, pointed straight at Rinaldo's head.

Deborah stood up, too, and gasped. "Primo!" she yelled. "Attack!" She let go of his leash, and he bounded in through the open window. Sofia screamed in shock as Primo charged at her legs. They buckled under her and she fell, the gun flying across the room.

Kat and Deborah rushed to climb through the window after Primo. Kat had carefully watched where the gun had landed. Rinaldo dashed for it, but she was faster. She backed into the corner of the room, pointing the gun at both Sofia and Rinaldo. "This ends now!" she shouted, wishing she knew how to speak Italian. Still, her meaning was quite clear.

They became still, Sofia on the floor, Rinaldo standing up. They were both panting with rage and from the heat of the argument.

Deborah grabbed her cell phone from her purse and shouted, *"Polizia!"* into it.

CHAPTER NINETEEN

It was a tense standoff. Kat didn't feel comfortable for a moment. She stood with the gun trained on Rinaldo, then on Sofia, then on Rinaldo again, while Primo growled and Deborah tugged on his collar to keep him under control.

"Why did you do it?" Kat asked.

Rinaldo ignored her and kept on cursing in Italian. Then he sunk into deep thought, and wouldn't say anything. Sofia continued to cry.

She kept asking Deborah what would happen. Would she be arrested? What about Diego? What would happen to him? Who would take care of him? Deborah translated it all for Kat.

Kat said she didn't know what would happen, but it was unlikely she'd be charged, since she knew nothing about the murder. She may be charged for pointing a gun at Rinaldo, but perhaps not. Kat decided she would vouch for her. Sofia, despite not being an angel, didn't know anything about her brother killing Bruno.

She obviously hadn't urged him on. She was innocent, and more than anything, Diego needed a mother. He'd lost his father and his uncle in one fell swoop. He would be left without any family if Sofia went to prison,.Of course, it would be up to the police to make the final decision, but Kat would stand up for her.

The police soon arrived, and arrested Rinaldo. Deborah explained everything to them. Thankfully they spoke English, and Kat told them all about Sofia, and how she didn't know anything about what had happened. Rinaldo was still in his own little world, and allowed himself to be led quietly away. He didn't say anything to Sofia, or about her, and the police left her in the house as they took Rinaldo away. She burst into tears all over again. Some other police came and took statements. It didn't take long and they were soon gone.

Deborah made coffee for the two of them, Sofia and Diego having gone to their rooms. They sipped it in the living room, the same room where all the drama had just unfolded. It felt so strange and eerie. Neither of them knew what to say. Primo curled up on the floor and fell asleep. His work was done.

After a short time, they heard a car pull into the driveway. Kat went to the window to see who it was, and saw Blaine and Luigi get out of the car. Deborah had called them. Blaine and Luigi both rushed to the door, and Kat rushed just as quickly to let them in.

Blaine grabbed Kat in a bear hug as soon as he entered, and Luigi said, "Deborah! Deborah!" She came running in, and they had a similar big bear hug. Deborah ended up crying on Luigi's shoulder, all of her adrenaline pouring out, as she began to comprehend the dangerous life-threatening situation they had just survived. She realized if Rinaldo, instead of Kat, had grabbed the gun, he probably would have killed all three of the women, and perhaps Diego as well.

"I was so, so worried about you," Luigi said. "I am so glad you're safe."

Kat, on the other hand, felt deeply satisfied. She snuggled into Blaine's chest, then looked up at him with a smile on her face. "It's all over now," she said.

Blaine smiled down at her, relief shining in his eyes. "I am so proud of you," he said, "but right now I'm asking the universe to not allow any murders to happen around you for at least another five years. My nerves just can't take it, honey."

Kat laughed. "If it's any consolation, I'm not sure mine can, either."

"Thank you so much," Luigi said to both of them. "Kat, your help has been invaluable. I am so indebted to you. Bruno can now rest in peace."

"Oh," Kat said modestly, "you're most welcome, but I didn't work alone. I couldn't have done it without Deborah."

"And neither of us could have done it without Primo," Deborah said. "He was wonderful. He bounded through the window and knocked the gun right out of Sofia's hand."

"Sofia had a gun?" Luigi asked.

Together they explained what had happened.

"And then Primo growled at Rinaldo, keeping him in line until the cops came," Kat said. "Who knows what would have happened without him?"

*****

The next morning, they all went to the Catholic church closest to the Lombardi estate for the funeral. Chiari was good friends with the priest there, and they had managed to arrange it on short notice.

It was a traditional Catholic funeral with last rites, a prayer vigil, funeral liturgy, and Catholic mass. All the mourners passed by the open casket, and kissed Bruno on his cold cheek.

After the funeral, they gathered outside for the burial. The entire graveyard was packed with people, since Bruno had been very popular. He had also given a lot of money to the local community, and everyone knew who he was. Even Sofia and Diego were present. Kat thought that was incredibly generous and big-hearted of Chiari to invite them. She wasn't sure she could have been as charitable if she'd found herself in the same situation.

Chiari had arranged a huge marble mausoleum for Bruno. She placed his favorite things in there – his Rolex watch, his cigars, some old family photos of his father, books, and, of course, plenty of wine. As each of the mourners passed, they placed a single rose or a handful of dirt on top of his casket.

There were some songs and prayers, and Chiari spoke from the heart about him.

When it drew to a close, Luigi, Deborah, Kat, and Blaine approached her.

"Thank you," she said in English, and hugged Kat. Then she hugged Deborah and kissed Luigi and Blaine on the cheeks. She turned to Deborah and said something in Italian. Deborah translated, "She says we are welcome to visit any time."

Kat said thank you, but wasn't sure she'd be back any time soon. As gorgeously beautiful as Sardinia was, with its mountains and beaches and glittering sea views, she'd need some time to not associate it with murder. She felt like she needed a vacation after this vacation.

She was in luck, because after they flew back to the Florence area she and Blaine would have some time in Florence before Deborah and Luigi's wedding and their return flight home to Kansas. She was ashamed to admit that after all the drama, she'd almost forgotten about Luigi and Deborah's wedding, the reason they'd come to Italy in the first place!

"We'll have to do this all over again sometime," Deborah said. "A day is just not enough to do all of Florence, trust me." But even so, they still had a wonderful time.

First they visited the Uffizi Gallery Museum. Kat loved its majestic courtyard, and time flew by as they wandered around, looking at the artworks. There were many of a religious nature, and Kat particularly liked the Filippo Lippi painting of Madonna with child and two angels. It was so intricate and detailed, especially the

Madonna's headdress. In contrast with all the excitement of the investigation, Kat felt deeply and utterly at peace.

Before lunch, they crossed the famous Ponte Vecchio bridge. It was very strange, with numerous shops set up on it, offering gold jewelry, souvenirs, and art pieces. Kat bought some lovely greetings cards and a writing set for Lacie. She struggled, trying to figure out what to buy for Tyler, but eventually settled on a belt made of quality Italian leather. Then she decided that Lacie's gift didn't look like enough, so she bought her a quality Italian leather handbag, too.

She liked the look of another handbag for herself, but it was in the Versace store on the way to the Florence Cathedral. It was black and white leather, absolutely sleek and gorgeous, without being too ostentatious. She peered at the price tag through the window. "A girl can dream," she said to Deborah, laughing, "but that's way out of my budget."

On their way to lunch, they went to the Florence Cathedral. When they stepped inside, it took Kat's breath away. The scale of it was just incredible, the vaulted ceiling towering so far up above it might as well have been the sky. Pillars with the circumference size of small houses reached all the way up to the top, the ceiling bridged with huge vaulted peaks. She could have spent hours looking at all the detailed frescoes, so incredibly intricate that she almost couldn't believe it. Reams of angels danced in the skies, while demons danced in hell, and humans were caught up in various states between it all.

They really packed in the sightseeing, and by the time it was 1:00 p.m., they were thoroughly tired out, and more than ready for lunch at an outdoor restaurant they selected. Kat sat there drinking her glass of wine. She looked around and felt incredibly happy, like the whole world was smiling down upon her.

"Thank you so much for showing us around," she said to Deborah and Luigi.

"You are more than welcome," Luigi said with a smile. "It has been an absolute pleasure. Besides, how could I possibly repay you for everything you've done for me? For Bruno?"

Kat smiled. "That was my pleasure. I'm just glad I was able to be of some help."

"We'd better get back, Luigi," Deborah said. "We need to make sure everything's ready for the wedding tomorrow."

"Yes," Luigi said.

"Do you need me to do anything?" Kat asked.

Deborah smiled. "I can handle it. Please, you two, stay in Florence. Enjoy yourselves to the maximum. Squeeze in every little bit of enjoyment you can before you have to leave."

So they did.

Deborah and Luigi returned to his estate in the Maybach which Luigi had driven from the airport. Kat and Blaine were to get a taxi when they were ready to return to Deborah's.

They wandered the streets of Florence, not going anywhere in particular. They held hands and strolled, deeply relaxed. Whenever they saw a shop they liked the look of, they ducked inside. An antique shop, a second-hand book store, a clothing store… Kat loved to window shop, and everything she saw was done with exquisite taste.

Kat couldn't remember the last time she'd been so completely and utterly happy. She and Blaine stopped at a gelateria. She had a coffee and mascarpone gelato combination, while Blaine opted for pear and cinnamon. They fed each other off the little spoons provided and watched people walk by.

Blaine laughed. "Well, it's not been the most relaxing vacation I've ever taken, but it's got to be the most eventful one."

"I'll say," said Kat with a smile. "Thank you for always supporting me. That really means a lot."

Blaine gave her a warm and loving smile. The one that still made her weak at the knees as his eyes crinkled. "That's my job, honey," he murmured.

CHAPTER TWENTY

The weather could not have been more perfect for a wedding. The ceremony took place under a grape-wrapped arbor on the front lawn of Luigi's massive castle, in the golden late-afternoon sunlight.

Like Deborah had alluded to, there was a huge turnout of Luigi's friends and business associates. Deborah herself just had Kat, Blaine, and Primo there, but she and Luigi were planning a visit to the States soon, so all of her friends in Lindsay and beyond could meet the love of her life.

Kat beamed with pride as she walked down the aisle just before the bride made her grand entrance. Deborah wore a blush colored two-piece lace over satin, that glimmered gorgeously in the afternoon sunlight. Kat wore a complementing dress in rose, which hugged her curves and made her feel like a million dollars. As she walked down the aisle, Deborah turned towards Kat and gave her a wide grin. Kat felt tears spring to her eyes, she was so happy Deborah was finally getting the wonderful life she deserved. She hoped beyond hope that Deborah and Luigi would have a long, happy life together.

Luigi stood at the altar next to his best man, a close childhood friend who had been recruited at the last minute to fill Bruno's spot. He had the biggest smile Kat thought she'd ever seen on anyone.

The ceremony was in Italian, but Kat didn't need to understand the words. She felt them and the deep, abiding love as Luigi and Deborah said their vows, exchanged rings, and shared their first kiss as a married couple. People burst into applause and cheers as they made their way back up the aisle. White and golden confetti burst into showers above their heads as the guests scattered it all over them. Even Primo who was tied by his leash to the last pew in the back of the church basked in the joy of the moment, barking happily.

Then they all went to the vineyard's tasting room for dinner.

Kat gasped as she stepped into the room. It was truly a banquet. There were huge long tables with white tablecloths, candelabras burning away, flickering shadows up against the stone walls. Staff stood at the edge of the room, next to an enormous table, packed to the brim with all kinds of foods.

Kat couldn't resist passing by the food table before she went to her seat at the head table beside Deborah. There were so many delicious dishes, she didn't know where to look first.

At the tables, they were served a choice of red wine, white wine and Prosecco, all from Luigi's estate. Next came the *antipasti* – plates and plates of mozzarella, charcuterie, almond-stuffed olives, fresh grilled anchovies, salads that looked nothing short of rainbows, focaccia, orange glazed bread, and just about anything else one could think of.

"Don't fill yourself up too much!" Deborah said. "There's plenty more to come!"

And she wasn't wrong. Next came the *primo piatto*. There was a choice between two dishes – ricotta and spinach ravioli, or *paccheri* with beef sauce. Kat was already feeling a little full from her ravioli, but she had to make more room for the main course. Again, there were two choices – guinea fowl with herb roasted potatoes and grilled asparagus, or lasagna – Deborah's absolute favorite – with an aragula salad. Kat had the lasagna and enjoyed it as much as Deborah did.

Sorbetta came next, a prosecco-lemon flavored sorbet. Kat thought it was dessert, but it just turned out to be a palate cleanser before the main dessert event. Kat went for the classic Tiramisu (she just couldn't get enough of it), but there was also an option of summer fruit and wild berry sauce on a caramelized biscuit base, with a marscarpone flavored gelato.

Soon, with everyone feeling as full as they'd ever been, the waiters went around and handed everyone a glass of Prosecco. Luigi stood up.

Deborah had to translate for Kat, and Kat was so glad she did, because Luigi's speech was so moving and heartfelt.

"Thank you to everyone for coming," he said. "Deborah and I are truly blessed to have so many people who wish us well and have come to celebrate our love. We appreciate that, from the bottom of our hearts.

"But everyone who knows me well will know that there's one very special guest who is missing. My best friend, Bruno Lombardi. Bruno and I met in Florence, both as young men, who were being advised by our fathers to get into the wine business. Advised... or should I say, pushed?"

Everyone laughed.

"From there, complaining about our respective fathers, we formed a life-long friendship. Bruno Lombardi was not a perfect man. Who among us is? But he was hilarious, and strong, and truly dedicated to his profession, no, his art, as a winemaker. He was charismatic, and could be cutthroat. He was a man of darkness and light, like us all, and owned his shortcomings well. He would call me out when I took the wrong path, and I would try to do the same for him.

"He should be here, standing next to me. But he is now... in the ground." A pained look touched Luigi's face. He bowed his head for a moment, then lifted it again. "But that cannot be changed. That has happened, and there is no secret way to be able to go back in time and change things.

"However, there is still a right way to do things. And the right way to do things in this instance was to get him justice. As his best friend, I knew he deserved that. The police... well, we all know about them."

Everyone laughed.

"While they can be wonderful, they may not always be. But friends? You know their heart is in the right place. My wonderful wife Deborah was involved in a murder investigation back in Lindsay, Kansas, where she comes from. And when the police failed to find the murderer, Kat Denham was the one who succeeded." He gestured toward Kat.

Kat, slightly taken aback, made a quick wave to the sea of people in front of them.

"She is not an investigator by profession. Rather, she is a talented writer, who creates new worlds with her pen. But her heart is made of gold, and she hates to see justice not being served. So she stepped up in Lindsay, Kansas, and solved the murder. Then – as if God still gave us a consolation after Bruno's death – she arrived just in time. Not one day after she had arrived, Bruno was murdered. And I thank God that she was here, and that she cannot rest until justice is done. Without hesitation, she decided to investigate. And she was entirely successful.

"My wonderful Deborah translated for her when the language barrier became too great, and Deborah's dog, Primo, offered aggression just when it was needed. The result was the arrest of the person responsible for Bruno's death. I could not be more grateful. Bruno's body may be in the ground, but his soul is now at peace as he has received justice, and he can go on to be with the Lord."

"Kat, thank you," he said in English. "And I hope that we can host you and your husband for many future times to come. In much happier times."

"Thank you," Kat said.

"We'd be most honored," said Blaine.

"And you're welcome to visit us in Lindsay any time," Kat added.

*****

While Deborah and Luigi stayed at his castle for the night, Blaine and Kat returned to Deborah's home for their last night, with Primo tagging along. He had grown to love Kat, and nuzzled his head against her knee in the taxi. She stroked him on his head. "Aww. I wish you could meet Jazz and Rudy. Perhaps Deborah will bring you along when she comes to visit us in Kansas."

The next day, the day they were due to leave, they awoke to something rather unexpected. Kat rubbed her eyes and opened the curtains to the balcony, and gasped.

"What is it?" Blaine said, concerned. He rushed to stand beside her, then his face broke into a huge smile. "Wow! These people..." He trailed off, speechless.

"So kind, aren't they?" Deborah said.

Out on the balcony, there was the most beautiful scene, right in front of their room. The empty balcony had been transformed, with gorgeous potted flowers, and an ornate white table with garlands woven around its legs. On the table, there was a huge spread of breakfast – coffee, prosecco, bread rolls, pastries of every kind, and a gorgeous array of brightly colored fruit. There was also a wrapped gift on the table.

Kat padded outside in her slippers, and then Luigi and Deborah came into view. They were a little way down the long balcony, watching Kat and Blaine with excitement, like little children spying on their parents.

Kat broke into a grin. "You two," she said as she pointed at them.

"You're spoiling us!"

"It is nothing," said Luigi. "Nothing can repay you for how you've helped us."

Blaine walked out of the bedroom, tying his robe and smiling. "This is really something."

"Open the present, open the present!" Deborah said excitedly, like a little kid.

"Okay," Kat said. She sat down at the table and unwrapped the gift, which was wrapped immaculately in white paper with a thick golden ribbon. As she opened it, she gasped. "Deborah, you didn't!"

Deborah grinned. "Yep, I did!"

Kat held up the gift to show Blaine. "The Versace bag you liked," he said. "Wow, Deborah, that's really generous of you."

"A gift for being the most wonderful matron of honor anybody could ever ask for," Deborah said. She came up behind Kat and gave her a big hug. "Thank you, Kat. For everything."

Kat got up and hugged her back. "You're so welcome. And thank you, too. I was so happy to be a part of your wedding."

They ate their farewell breakfast together, looking over Deborah's garden and her small "starter" vineyard beyond.

"It's a shame you didn't get to do more in Florence, and see Siena, and all the other amazing things we'd planned on doing," Deborah said.

"Well, we got to see a lot of Sardinia, and that was such a beautiful island," Kat said. "Maybe next time we'll do all the rest."

Luigi grinned. "Does that mean you're not put off for life?"

"Not at all." Kat said. "Not in the slightest. I'm a bit tougher than that, thank you, Luigi." she teased. Everyone laughed.

Soon it was time for them to leave. Luigi drove in the Maybach, while Deborah came along for the ride. When Kat was saying goodbye to Primo on the driveway, he whined and cried so much that Deborah said he could come along too, and say goodbye at the airport like the rest of them.

At the airport, everyone hugged. Kat knelt down and ruffled Primo's head.

"We'll see you soon," Blaine said. "First in Kansas, then back here. Luigi, we'll do some great golf when you come to Lindsay."

Luigi gave him another handshake that led to a manly pat on the back sort of hug. "You got it."

"Bye, Deborah," Kat said. "Thank you for everything, and the bag."

Deborah gave her a lovely smile. "You're worth it."

EPILOGUE – SIX MONTHS LATER

Salvatore handed Alessa the keys to the B and B. He smiled. Alessa hadn't seen him smile very often. "These are for you," he said. "You have done such an incredible job, and you deserve to have them."

Alessa smiled. They were at Gianna's bar and she was sipping on a Coke. "Thank you," she said. "I'd love to continue being the manager."

Salvatore grinned at his companion. "No," he said. "Not the manager. The manager and the owner."

Alessa's smile disappeared, to be replaced by total and utter shock. "No… What? You mean… Seriously?"

Salvatore and his companion laughed. "Yes. Seriously." he said. "The B and B is all yours. You are the one who has loved it back to life. Now, take it. Keep it forever. Cherish it."

Alessa broke down and cried. "Oh my goodness. Oh, Sal, this is too much. Sal, you are too generous."

"No," he said. "You helped me so much when I was depressed. Not only with making the B and B beautiful, but by helping to heal my heart. I owe you much more than this, Alessa. More than you'll ever know."

Tears were running down Alessa's face. She smiled, speechless.

"But don't worry," Salvatore said cheerfully. He put his arm around his companion, Chiari. "Chiari and I will come and visit often." He winked. "You can prepare us the finest suite."

They all laughed, knowing there were no fine suites in the B and B.

"And of course, you will be an honored guest at our wedding," Chiari said.

*****

It was the best day of Lorenzo's working life. He clutched the magazine to his chest, and ran from his office to the salon, where Vito was drinking a glass of his own wine, a raft of papers stretched across the coffee table, where he was planning for next year's releases.

"Mr. Rizzo," he said, bursting into the room. "Look at this. You placed 1st in the wines of the year!"

"Oh ha ha," Vito said, not looking up. "Of course the Lombardi estate would…"

"No," Lorenzo said, rushing over and thrusting the magazine at him. "Look. 1st place in the wines of the year… from the Rizzo winery!"

Vito skimmed the magazine, then threw it victoriously in the air. "Yes!" He grabbed Lorenzo and embraced him in a huge bear hug, the first time he'd ever done so. "Yes, yes, yes!" Then he dug into his pocket and pulled out his wallet. He didn't even bother counting the money, just fished out a thick wad of bills and slapped it into Lorenzo's hand. "Go. Take your wife and kids on holiday for two weeks, and I don't want to hear anything from you during that time. Go, take a cruise, fly to America, go to England and see the Queen… anything you like!"

"Oh, sir," Lorenzo said, incredibly taken aback. "Are you… are you sure?"

"Yes. Now get out of her before I change my mind."

"Thank you, sir, thank you so much!" Lorenzo hurried into the office, grabbed his briefcase, and jumped into his car, excitement exploding inside his chest. He couldn't remember the last time he'd been on a vacation with his family or relaxing with his family, without Vito calling him and demanding that he attend to something.

As hee drove home, his mind filled with the images of his children's faces smiling up at him. Life was good.

*****

Rinaldo sat in his cell, thinking about how his life had gone so wrong. He'd been certain that Gabriele would be arrested for the murder, but Rinaldo realized maybe he wasn't as smart as he'd thought he was. The police chief had gotten a search warrant for his home and found evidence of thallium. After much interrogation, Rinaldo admitted that a chemist friend of his who worked at a scientific laboratory in Florence had obtained it for him.

The friend had no idea what he was going to do with it. Rinaldo had simply said he was playing a joke on a friend. He wanted it because it was odorless, colorless, and tasteless. In other words, the perfect poison to put in a bottle of wine. The deadly effects were instant. Rinaldo's plan had worked.

But his 'getting away with it' plan had definitely not worked. Now he was facing a lifetime in jail. No future. No hope. All he could do was get on his knees every day and beg God, Jesus, Mother Mary and whoever else would listen, for forgiveness.

*****

"Well, who knew I would be finding love at the school gate?" Sofia said happily to her sister. She was standing in front of a mirror fixing her hair, her telephone call to her sister on speakerphone. She had been really close to her sister as a child, but as adults they'd drifted apart. Only now, since Bruno had died and Rinaldo had been locked up, had they rekindled their friendship.

Despite it being hard to get over Bruno, she had started to take on some of what Rinaldo had said, especially since her sister was echoing it. "You deserve to be a man's one and only," her sister had said. "Make sure to never get involved with a man with attachments like that again. You want someone who's free and single and can show your beautiful self off to the world."

Diego had a friend at school, Francisco, who had a little crush on Sofia. Turned out, his single father had a crush on her as well. Little Francisco blabbed all about it when he came over to play on the gaming console. "My father thinks you are very beautiful, Ms. Ossani," he said. "He said your eyes sparkle, and you have a lovely smile." The poor man would have been mortified if he found out what his son had said.

But that afternoon when he came to pick up Francisco, Sofia looked at him in a new way. Previously she'd only had eyes for Bruno. But now? Well, there was certainly something about the light in his eyes, and the way he looked when he smiled. Perhaps something could happen…

Francisco burst the bubble. "I told Ms. Ossani you think she's beautiful, dad."

He looked like he wanted the ground to swallow him up. "I'm so sorry, Ms. Ossani."

She smiled at him. "It's okay."

A couple of playdates later, he'd plucked up the courage to ask her on a date.

So here she was, in front of the mirror, fixing her hair, getting ready to go out with him. Diego was going to go with them over to Francisco's house, and the boys would stay at home, while Sofia and

Giorgio would meander down the road to the local bar. Giorgio's wife had left the family a few years ago, and he was very much a single man.

Sofia smiled at herself in the mirror. She just knew it was going to be a beautiful night.

*****

Kat and Blaine were in bed, lights on, sitting up. Kat had been editing her latest manuscript, ready to write draft two, while Blaine was reading a book. He made it a principle never to bring work to bed.

Kat's phone beeped. "It's Deborah. She's sent me a WhatsApp message." She took the phone and showed Blaine the pictures. There was one of Primo, one of a couple Kat vaguely recognized in front of Deborah's house, and a lovely one of Luigi and Deborah on the veranda of their castle-like home with the panoramic view shown behind them.

"I've rented my home and vineyard to Gregory and Tara Ralph. Do you remember them? They were both veterinarians in a nearby town and came from Italy to do lectures for students at Lindsay University. They're retiring now. They always wanted to try their hand at winemaking, and they decided this was their chance. I've moved into Luigi's castle, and we're very happy here. Can't wait to see you soon."

Kat replied, then looked at Blaine.

"I can't wait to see them either. But... now that we've gotten a taste of somewhat exotic travel, where do you think we should go next?"

"London," Blaine said. "There are so many historic things to see."

"Yes. Great idea," said Kat. "I want to go to Paris, too. And Rome. What about Greece? Portugal?"

Blaine laughed. "You'll be doing a round-the-world cruise next."

"That's a great idea," Kat said. "I'll look them up right now on my phone."

"Oh no you don't," Blaine said with a laugh. "You'll have to remortgage your house first."

Kat laughed along, then lay down and snuggled into Blaine. "I can't wait to explore the world with you."

He stroked her hair. "I can't think of anyone else I'd rather do it with."

RECIPES

PANCETTA WRAPPED ASPARAGUS

Ingredients:
1 lb. asparagus stalks, bottoms trimmed
4 slices pancetta (It's okay to substitute thinly sliced bacon.)
2 tbsp. butter, melted
¼ tsp. garlic powder
1 tsp. brown sugar
¼ tsp. freshly ground pepper

Directions:
Preheat oven to 400 degrees. Divide the asparagus into four bundles. Tightly wrap one slice of pancetta around each bundle. In a small bowl, combine the butter, garlic powder, brown sugar, and pepper.

Arrange the asparagus bundles on a baking sheet and drizzle the butter mixture over the top. Bake for 25-30 minutes or until the pancetta is crisp. Enjoy!

ARINCINI (ITALIAN RICE BALLS)

Ingredients:
1 tbsp. olive oil
1 small onion, finely chopped
1 clove garlic, finely crushed
1 cup Arborio rice (Make sure you use Arborio and not another variety.)
½ cup dry white wine
2 ½ cups boiling chicken stock
½ cup frozen green peas
2 oz. finely chopped ham
Salt and freshly ground pepper to taste
½ cup finely grated Parmesan cheese
1 egg, beaten
1 egg
1 tbsp. milk
4 oz. mozzarella cheese, cut into ¾" cubes
½ cup all-purpose flour
1 cup dry bread crumbs
1-quart vegetable oil for deep fat frying

Directions:
Heat olive oil in a large saucepan over medium heat. Add onion and garlic and cook, stirring often until onion is soft. Pour in the rice and cook, stirring, for 2 minutes, then stir in the wine and continue cooking and stirring until the liquid has evaporated. Add hot chicken stock to the rice 1/3 cup at a time, stirring and cooking until the liquid has evaporated before adding more.

When the chicken stock has all been added and the liquid has evaporated, stir in the peas and ham. Season with salt and pepper. Remove from the heat and stir in the Parmesan cheese. Transfer the risotto to a bowl and allow to cool slightly.

Stir the beaten egg into the risotto. In a small bowl, whisk the remaining egg and milk with a fork. For each ball, roll 2 tablespoons of the risotto into a ball. Press a piece of the mozzarella cheese into the center and roll to enclose. Coat lightly with flour, dip into the milk mixture, then roll in bread crumbs to coat.

Heat oil for frying in a deep saucepan to 350 degrees. Fry the balls in small batches until evenly golden, turning as needed. Drain on paper towels. Keep warm in low oven while the rest are frying. Enjoy!

INSALATA CAPRESE

Ingredients:
4 large ripe tomatoes, sliced ¼" thick
1 lb. fresh mozzarella cheese, sliced ¼" thick
1/3 cup fresh basil leaves
3 tbsp. extra virgin olive oil
Fine sea salt to taste
Freshly ground black pepper to taste
½ cup pitted black olives

Directions:
On a large platter, alternate and overlap the tomato slices, mozzarella cheese slices, and basil leaves. Scatter with the olives and then drizzle with olive oil. Season with salt and pepper.

TAGLIATELLE AL RAGÙ ALLA BOLOGNESE

Ingredients:
1 pkg. fresh or dry tagliatelle
¼ lb. pancetta
½ lb. stewing beef, cubed
½ lb. pork shoulder, cubed
2 medium onions, peeled
2 medium carrots, peeled
2 celery stalks
½ cup butter + ¼ cup butter
4 tbsp. olive oil

5 cups (2 cans) canned chopped Italian tomatoes, drained
1 cup dry white wine
Salt and freshly ground pepper to taste
Freshly grated nutmeg to taste
1 ½ cups warm beef broth
1 ½ cups heavy cream
Grated Parmesan cheese to taste

Directions:

Place the pancetta, beef, and pork in the freezer. When semi-frozen, cut them into narrow strips then freeze the strips. This makes them easier to cut. When frozen, mince with a knife. Set aside.

Finely chop the onions, carrots, and celery stalks. Heat ½ cup butter and oil in a heavy based pot over medium heat. When the butter is melted add the chopped vegetables and the meats. Sauté for 10 minutes.

Press drained tomatoes through a sieve into a bowl. Add the wine into the meat and vegetable mixture. Let it rest for 5 minutes. Add the tomatoes and simmer for 20 minutes. Season to taste with salt, pepper, and nutmeg, then add the beef broth. Cover the pot and simmer for 45 minutes, stirring occasionally with a wooden spoon. Add the cream, mix well, lower the heat and reduce uncovered for 25 minutes.

When ready to serve, bring a large pot of water to a boil. Add salt to taste. When water boils, cook the tagliatelle according to package instructions.

Place ¼ cup butter in a large, warmed serving bowl and put it over the pot of boiling water to melt the butter. When ready, drain the pasta and transfer the pasta to the bowl. Mix well with the butter then pour the sauce over it. Mix and serve immediately with grated Parmesan on the side. Enjoy!

ORANGE BREAD LOAF

Ingredients:
2 oranges, scrubbed
1 stick unsalted butter + 2 tsp. for loaf pan, softened
1 ¾ cups all-purpose flour
1 ½ tsp. baking powder
½ tsp. Kosher salt
1 ½ cups sugar
2 eggs + 1 egg yolk
1 cup ricotta cheese

Directions:
Preheat oven to 350 degrees. Grate 2 tbsp. orange zest. Juice the oranges. Butter a 9" x 5" x 3" loaf pan. Whisk together flour, baking powder, and salt. Drop butter into the bowl of a stand mixer. On medium-high, beat until fluffy, stopping to scrape sides. Add 1 cup sugar and beat until fluffy. Add the eggs, egg yolk, and ricotta cheese and beat until fluffy. Add flour and beat on low to combine.

Scrape batter into prepared pan and smooth the top. Bake until cake is golden brown and a toothpick comes out crumb-flecked, approximately 55-60 minutes. Let cool for 10 minutes.

While cake cooks, make the glaze. Pour ½ cup sugar into a saucepan and add ¾ cup orange juice. Simmer until sugar dissolves and syrup thickens, about 3 minutes. Remove cake from pan and set on a rack over a baking sheet. Brush glaze over warm loaf. When cake is cool, slice and serve. Enjoy!

Paperbacks & Ebooks for FREE

Go to www.dianneharman.com/freepaperback.html and get your FREE copies of Dianne's books and favorite recipes immediately by signing up for her newsletter.

Once you've signed up for her newsletter you're eligible to win three paperbacks. One lucky winner is picked every week. Hurry before the offer ends!

ABOUT THE AUTHOR

Dianne lives in Huntington Beach, California, with her husband, Tom, a former California State Senator, and her boxer dog, Kelly. Her passions are cooking, reading, and dogs, so whenever she has a little free time, you can either find her in the kitchen, playing with Kelly in the back yard, or curled up with the latest book she's reading.

Her award winning books include:

Cedar Bay Cozy Mystery Series

Cedar Bay Cozy Mystery Series - Boxed Set

Liz Lucas Cozy Mystery Series

Liz Lucas Cozy Mystery Series - Boxed Set

High Desert Cozy Mystery Series

High Desert Cozy Mystery Series - Boxed Set

Northwest Cozy Mystery Series

Northwest Cozy Mystery Series - Boxed Set

Midwest Cozy Mystery Series

Midwest Cozy Mystery Series - Boxed Set

Jack Trout Cozy Mystery Series

Cottonwood Cozy Mystery Series

Coyote Series

Midlife Journey Series

Red Zero Series

Newsletter

If you would like to be notified of her latest releases please go to www.dianneharman.com and sign up for her newsletter.

Website: www.dianneharman.com,
Blog: www.dianneharman.com/blog
Email: dianne@dianneharman.com